Secrets of Ba

The Curious Adventures Of The Real Holmes And Watson

The Daring Escapes of a Doctor and A Detective

The tales scribed here are the recollections of I, Doctor John Watson, from my recollections, notes, and records kept in my diaries when I lived in the residence 221B Baker Street with my companion, Sherlock Holmes. Sherlock was always quite keen on my record keeping; she insisted I did our adventures the justice they deserved.

Orange Pip Books.

Paperback ISBN 978-1-78705-799-9

ePub ISBN 978-1-78705-800-2

PDF ISBN 978-1-78705-801-9

Published by Orange Pip Books

335 Princess Park Manor, Royal Drive, London, N11 3G

www.orangepipbooks.com

Cover design by Brian Belanger
Cover illustration by Jamie Simpson

Contents

To all the incredible, strong women in my life. Thank you for giving me strength.

The Rooms at 221B Baker Street

It was clear to me from a young age I could not accomplish all I wanted to with the gender assigned to me at birth. My father reportedly wept when my dear mother brandished a girl from the theatre at Chelmsford's hospital. In my later years, I concluded that the wave of emotion was bitter disappointment. Of course, when my brother Harris appeared the following year, my father forgave my impudence for being born female and I was sent away to finishing school.

Looking out onto the hotel's dining hall on the Strand, I pondered of my father and wondered what he would think of me now. I had not turned out the way he had longed for me to. There was no graceful, married lady here - the only things my mother and I shared were our fair hair and full lips.

The dining space was filled with couples in their morning attire. Ladies dressed in embroidered petticoats that were buttoned up to their chins to help them cope with the September weather. I shivered at the thought of being tied in one of the contraptions that were women's corsets as I had been at school. Naturally, I loathed being sent away, and found such tasks as embroidery, fan-waving, and learning to keep house to be menial activities. I lived in books. I snuck myself into classes in biology, physics, and chemistry, and studied relentlessly.

The butlers had noted my usual morning lateness and had prepared me a table by the window. I was presented with a pot of tea and a jug of milk whilst my breakfast was prepared. My brother had written to me about how Americans had curious sugared treats for their morning meal. The thought of him brought about a pang in my chest as I realised how much I missed him.

My brother had indulged my curious, studious mind and brought me books from his college where he had been studying the medical sciences from a young age. We often spoke in jest about swapping roles – much to my father's chagrin.
Father was determined to keep my brother in the family business of becoming a doctor like him. Everything was set and ready. I was to conclude my studies at a finishing school in Winchester, and my brother was to become a doctor.

However, the only thing dear Harris loathed more than my father was studying.

"My loveliest, loneliest sister," he declared one morning as he came into my suite in our family house in Chelmsford. "How does a flower-like you thrive in the world of education?"

I had crossed my legs under my dress and had a physiology book open in my lap. My notes were fanned out all around me in the moleskin notebooks I kept in prim condition.
"One cannot be bored when there is so much to be learned," I replied, gesturing for him to leave so I could enjoy the engagement of academia once more. "You should be joyous for you are blessed with the freedom of masculinity."

Harris leaned against the doorframe and crossed his arms; his green eyes were bright and full of mischief on his tanned face. Our father was out providing terror with every domestic visit on his round, no doubt. I shut the book. For I knew since we had the house to ourselves – a plot must be afoot.

That day my brother and I struck a deal. He would write to the finishing school on my father's behalf – as he frequently kept the surgery's correspondences and knew his hand – informing them of an illness that was preventing me to study there. I would instead fill my brother's position at his school, posing as John Watson, his younger brother. With a neat forgery from my brother, complete with the assurance of my father's continued donations to St. Bartholomew's Hospital in London, I was all set.

My brother decided that, with his newfound freedom, he would go and visit our Aunt in New York. She was a flamboyant widow in need of an heir. Harris was confident that he would be able to win her over. After all, our mother's sister had a soft spot for the "lonely lambs" of England.

My father's declining health meant he no longer travelled and had nurses in residence as I started my practice in St Bartholomew's. I learned quickly how to cover my female visage with stage makeup and male clothing. Both I found rather liberating – especially the absence of a corset.

My father passed away as I started at the University of London. I knew he thought me a disappointment thus the loss didn't ail me as perhaps it should have. I did not attend the funeral either, despite paying for it. I'd made peace with his death long before it happened. My brother divided the inheritance among us from his new home in New York and I was blessed with considerable income to fund my studies. I lived a secret life in London as John – Johanna making an appearance only in the most private of evenings spent alone until I graduated in 1874.

I joined the Army as a result of some friends of mine signing up to offer their services to queen and country. However, I was injured on my first tour, struck with enteric fever, and was returned home. With my nerves shaken beyond imagination, my only desire was to do nothing but sleep.

I had taken up residence in a hotel on the Strand while I decided what my next move should be. I could return to my practice. Maybe I could travel? Perhaps London was not my place to be anymore? Truthfully, my fingers itched to be back with patients. But maybe my gifts had been retired too long and I might have lost my skills. The thought waned on my mind. Nothing seemed like the correct move for me anymore.

I found myself staring at the teapot. A familiar voice pulled me from the bleakness of my thoughts.
"Dear God, Watson, is that you?" came from the table opposite. I looked up and saw dear old Stamford, a friend of mine from St Bartholomew's. I smiled widely. It never failed to amuse me that so many of my closest friends and allies all believed I was born a brother and not a sister.

"Stamford!" I exclaimed. He came over at once. "Goodness, Watson – thin as a reed. Are you well, man?" I gestured to the seat in front of me and he sat down, resting a mahogany topped cane on the arm of the seat. "Quite well," I said, folding the broadsheet back up and resting it on the side of the table. "How are you fairing? I heard you moved up from being a dresser at the hospital," I replied. I had lost weight since my time on the front, though it seemed the least of my worries. My companions all had jobs and a means of moving forward. Many spread out over fair England, some even residing further afield in the beauty of Wales or the hills of Scotland.

"Ah, the times have not been kind to men of our profession, Watson," he said, a wary smile on his round face. His hair seemed to have been shrinking back to his ears as it did for men of a certain age. I was fortunate – baldness in women was not that common. He asked the serving gentleman for a pot of his own tea as my bacon, eggs, and porridge arrived. "I may have been promoted in my profession, but the days are long and tiresome, Watson." He said with a sigh. I remembered him being distinctly smitten with the pastime of complaining.

I let my mind drift as he told me of the newfound woes of his blossoming career. I had no qualms with him, yet I found that my worries must've furrowed my brow. Stamford halted his tirade. Thankfully, he had not got onto the subject of his wife yet. A dear thing she was, too.

"Your countenance has fallen, John," he remarked, looking at me with his close brown eyes and sticking out his chin. He rubbed his stubbled jaw where he kept a trimmed beard and a buoyant moustache. "Enough about me. Tell me what is bothering you so?"

I finished off my breakfast and shook my head briskly.

"Nothing is amiss, Stamford," I replied. "Only worries that will melt once I have solved their problems." I swept the broadsheet I had originally prepared to be my company off the

9

table. "You are lucky to have crossed my path today," I followed as he sipped his tea, "I shall not be staying here much longer." Stamford swallowed as he placed the cup on the saucer once more. "I am looking for rooms in London – but I have not found much that is not by any means agreeable."

Ever since returning from service I had wallowed in my rooms here on the Strand, living a comfortable existence on my eleven shillings a week, supplemented by the money I had remaining from my inheritance. However, I would need to be more frugal to continue to live with basic comforts.

"I know of a man," Stamford said, resting his elbows on the table as he spoke animatedly. "He is a unique sort of fellow – a researcher... I believe. An acquaintance that I met at the hospital. He has found some rooms in Baker Street, but was looking for a gent to share the space with so he could afford it."

I knew Baker Street to be a great central locale – close to the station and the surrounding amenities. It sounded perfect. My reply was instant.

"That sounds most aggregable," I replied tapping the table with my palm, "I must meet this man at once." The sudden arrangement for my day gave me a rush that had been long begotten by my system. Stamford regarded me strangely for a moment before nodding. I readied myself to leave by throwing my coat over my shoulders.

"Of course, of course," he said finishing his tea and doing the same. "I must warn you," he added talking with a lilted tone. "He is an odd sort of man."

I shrugged my shoulders. The men I served beside in the army surely could be no stranger mix of weird and worn. "Perhaps I know him?" I proposed as he led the way to the door. "Tell me his name?" Stamford's reply was quick. "Sherlock Holmes."

Stamford led me, at once, to the familiar halls at Bartholomew's hospital, his colleagues all regarded him with kindness and me with curiosity for it had been many years since I had served there. The familiar smell of bromine and rubbing alcohol brought back many memories of patched-up soldiers in the field hospital beside me.

"Does he work in the archives?" I asked as we walked down two flights of stairs. Stamford sighed.

"No, John," he replied. "I daresay he will be in the morgue conducting another strange experiment." The lights dipped and a glow of paraffin oil lamps lit the way between the doors of the morgue. My curiosity was piqued.

"Not a Victor Frankenstein, I hope?" Stamford loosed a laugh.
"I wouldn't put it past him," his voice echoed down the hall as we drew up at the familiar door of the morgue. Stamford rapped his fist twice against the door.

"In but *quickly!*" a stern voice called back. Stamford immediately pushed the door open wide. The smell was the first thing to hit me – it made my eyes sting. A mist of blackish-green filled the subterranean room. "Sulphur – Stamford!" he declared over from the other end of the morgue.

Stamford immediately pulled out his handkerchief and pressed it against his nose. I did the same with mine.

The figure at the end of the morgue was remarkably tall. He had thrown his coat over one of the spare mortician tables, and I spotted a hat and cane hastily cast aside over another one. The sleeves of his white shirt were drawn up to their elbows and a great pair of black gloves covered his hands. His dark waistcoat was drawn around a slim waist from black corduroy breeches. The black bowtie he wore was askew.

"Yes, yes, yes!" the gentleman exclaimed. "I have got it!" Stamford fanned about to disperse the smoke. "Sherlock, what is this?" As the image around us grew clearer I spotted what remained of a body on a nearby table. The arm was singed black at the bone, the fingers blue with age. The rest of the body, however, was missing.

"Gunpowder!" Sherlock exclaimed. A dark woollen scarf muffled his voice as he had it tied around his mouth – for protection, no doubt. "I was testing the effectiveness of using it as a form of ignition to destroy a body. And it's many forms." He was speaking quite rapidly. If I didn't concentrate, I would miss the words. "Most informative!" he declared, clapping his hands together. Stamford and I shared a look of confusion.

"Who have you brought to see me, Stamford?" he turned to us after a moment. The bright grey eyes on his face caught mine and creased in the corners. Sherlock Holmes pulled down the scarf covering his chin and a wide smile graced their lips. "Who might you be, sir? Friend or foe?"

12

Stamford took the handkerchief from his lips, tentatively sucked in air, and then bundled it back in his pocket. I lowered mine too – it tasted bitter, filled with a pungent burnt aroma. Neither of those things seemed to bother Mr Holmes.

"Mr Holmes, allow me to introduce my friend, Mr John Watson," Stamford said, standing to the side. I outstretched a hand, and Holmes shook it firmly. He had an oval-shaped face with a sharp chin. Dark hair framed his pale skin. His moustache was trimmed, sideburns neat. Looking at him, he must've been quite the outsider to not have been married already. "He too is looking for lodging in London."

"Ah, excellent, Stamford," Sherlock exclaimed. "I've been having trouble finding someone suitable for a time now." His eyes shone with a welcome happiness that I was not at all expecting. "Tell me, Doctor," Sherlock began. "Do you have any troublesome habits that I should be aware of? Drinking? Gambling?"
"No, Sir," I replied. "Only that I am a miserable git in the mornings and rise when I want to." This made Stamford laugh heartily. The corner of Sherlock's lips quirked. "What about yourself, Holmes?" I continued.

Sherlock pressed his lips together and considered for a moment. "I do smoke shag tobacco quite often," he declared. "Would that bother you?" He seemed to be teasing me – or perhaps I was imagining it? I shook my head. "How about violin playing?" he added.

"That depends on the mastery of the player," I replied, sticking my chin out. I would not be intimidated by this man. Sherlock tilted his head to the side.

"That will not be a problem, Doctor," he replied, a little arrogantly.

"How did you know John was a doctor?" Stamford suddenly butted in. I had almost forgotten he was there during Holmes and Its exchange. "I never said."

Sherlock gave us a humble smile then.

"My dear Stamford," he said in a quick voice. "Look at the way this *person* stands." He added, I suddenly became aware of many eyes on my being. "His coat is from Garibaldi's in the market in Notting Hill – a well-to-do gentleman would be happy with such a coat. But this is an old one – suggesting that he is a well-off gentleman, but is out of practice of his trade," Sherlock said. "His hands are not calloused enough for a physical trade such as carpentry or metalwork. He speaks with a north-country tinge too. Where no doubt a doctor would be more valued than a lawyer or a governor."

When he finished, I found myself struck dumb by the assumptions Sherlock had made. He had barely shared a space with me for ten minutes and had concluded all this from a meeting as scarce as this. As Stamford exclaimed a cry of laughter and disbelief, my chest tightened. How much more could have this fellow gathered from his analysis?

I rejected the thought – no one had noticed thus far in however many years it had been. Surely, this odd-ball couldn't have seen through me. I gave Sherlock my most confident smile.

"That was quite a few assumptions, Holmes," I replied. His piercing grey eyes shone as he smiled. "That was spot on!" Stamford conceded beside me, clapping his hands at the marvel. "Holmes, you are a genius." Sherlock brushed the compliment aside with a flick of his hand.

"Only a consulting detective," Sherlock replied but there was a look of pride on his face. "Deductions are my trade, Watson," he added, "I've been told I am rather good at them."

"I don't doubt it, sir," I replied in a voice as light as I could muster. Sherlock appeared unfazed. "Shall we meet tomorrow at noon to view the rooms? I daresay you will find them quite satisfactory for your activities."

"That sounds perfect." He shook my hand again and we shared our farewells.

I could feel his grey eyes focused on the back of my head as we left.

Stamford and I shared the afternoon together in Hyde Park before the light of day drew to evening and he left me in the foyer at my hotel. Stamford had done little but distract me from my fraying nerves.

Sherlock seemed to be sharper than a razor blade – could I risk living with a person like him? My mind ran over the possible consequences and ramifications of being exposed. The life that I had worked so diligently to create could crumble around me.

Yet this Sherlock seemed to have created a name for himself as somewhat of an eccentric all on his own. Perhaps he wouldn't be taken seriously. Stamford marvelled at his skills like he was a God of his own – but he was only one man. I resolved to go and view the rooms and make my own inspection when Sherlock and I were alone.

Baker Street was all a bustle when I arrived a little before noon, but 221B ostensibly sat a great deal away from the noise and general mayhem of the roads. As I approached the house, I was surprised to see Sherlock was there already, a pipe blowing clouds of smoke into the air. He drew it away from his lips and waved as I approached.

"I am glad to see my feeling about you was correct, Watson," he said with a smile that I recognised with the same smugness from yesterday. I gave him a polite smile. "Another deduction, Holmes?" came my reply. He shook his head and lead the way.

"A guess," he said as we ascended the stairs up to a dark wooden door. Sherlock rapped on the door twice, removing his cap. I did the same with my bowler. A short, plump older woman opened the door. She had curled dark hair and wore a simple afternoon dress in grey, with bishop sleeves and an apron tied around her midsection. She gave us both a wide smile.

"Mr Holmes! How pleasant it is to see you again," she exclaimed as she let the pair of us in. She shook Sherlock's hand first and then mine. I noticed the aged tinge of a former Glaswegian accent. "And you have brought a companion!"

"Mrs Hudson, your charm is ever resplendent," Sherlock said, stepping aside. The house smelled like flowers and wax as if she had been burning lavender candles. I spotted a row of paintings on the wall that I didn't recognize – perhaps done by her own hand. "I'll let my esteemed colleague present himself."

"Doctor John Watson, ma'am," I replied. Her cheerful brown eyes shone. "A doctor," she exclaimed. She led Sherlock and me up the stairs to the apartment above her own. I heard the jangle of keys. "I do hope you like the space – a doctor on the property could be very convenient, indeed."

"Are you well, ma'am?" I asked, to which she and Sherlock laughed. I wondered how long the pair had known each other.

"My only sickness is age, sir," she said as the door opened with a creak into a light room. "One no doctor can fix, I'm afraid."

The apartment consisted of a living room leading into a kitchen, two bathrooms and two bedrooms of considerable size. The walls were papered with a dark poppy and bloom pattern on the walls of the living space. There were burgundy-coloured drapes and two high-backed green armchairs.

It was a very clean, well-furnished space – ideal for the pair of us. I could envision myself sitting close to the fire on a cold day with a book on my lap. It had a certain modern charm and a professional edge to it that made me understand

17

why my new companion liked it so. Plus, Mrs Hudson seemed very agreeable too. My reservations for Holmes aside, I knew that this would a deal I could not afford to miss. I had missed the privacy of my own quarters in my own abode – surely this step would alleviate the illogical fears I had of discovery.

By the end of the day, the deal was complete. I took a taxi from the hotel with my belongings the following morning. Mrs Hudson informed me that Sherlock had called the telephone and reported that he would arrive tomorrow.

I made myself at home in the south bedroom facing the garden. Sherlock had wanted the one facing the road – no doubt it would have better sun. However, I knew I would prefer the tranquillity of the greenery outside, the sway of the flowers in the small patch of garden made for a peaceful viewing.

I arranged my collection of things around my new room. My books barely filled one of the shelves. I had a few of my brother's letters kept in a locked box which I placed on my desk next to my old doctor's notes. I had kept some other precious items locked away in storage – mainly to protect them from my mother. That evening, Baker Street was peaceful. For once it didn't take me long to fall asleep.

The next morning, I awoke to the noise of violin music. My heart jumped into my throat as I got up. I only wore my cotton pyjamas and was glad that I had locked my door last night. I didn't sleep with my fake moustache and beard on, nor did I bind my chest at night so that it lay flat like a man's. It would be inconvenient to sleep with all my theatrical attire – and quite uncomfortable, I'd imagine – as it would move about as I slumbered. I now combed my hair and applied the stage makeup.

Opening the door, I saw the back of Sherlock Holmes poised with a mahogany violin, playing a beautiful morning tune. Of course, he played at a professional level.

"I wondered what time you would make it here, Holmes," I said. He turned around. The morning light caught in their hair. It wasn't combed neatly – thick, dark hair fell over their head. Those stunning grey eyes were set with a mischievous gleam.

"I do attempt to keep track of time," Holmes said. "I just put the kettle on the stove. Tea?" he said. "Please." I took a seat on the armchair closest to the window.

"How is it you enjoy rising late?" Holmes asked as he disappeared into the kitchen.

"I have no plans," I replied. "Why should I not enjoy peace when it is granted to me?"

"I don't suppose a charlatan such as yourself does have many plans these days?" Holmes' voice rose above the whistle of the kettle. My heart stilled in my chest.

"You jest, Holmes though I fear I have not grasped it," I replied. His footsteps returned quickly with a delicate cup and saucer.

"It is very hard for me," he said slowly, placing the tea in front of me, "*not* to notice something."

I took the saucer and sipped. I'd planned this many times in my mind already and had conjured forty-thousand lines to deal with such a scenario.

"I don't know what you mean, Holmes."

Sherlock sat opposite me.

"Don't fret, Watson. You are safe here." His voice softened before taking a long draw of his tea. I placed my cup down, crossing my arms.

"I should hope so," I replied with a chuckle. We could laugh this whole ordeal off and then pray he never speaks of it again. "I'm afraid I truly don't know what you mean, Holmes."

Sherlock balanced the cup on his knee as he tilted his head to the left.

"It's quite alright, miss. "I have no qualms with women." He grinned as a faintness overtook me. My gaze fell to the carpeted floor and the pattern that seemed to be swimming around me. I was glad for being sat down.

"In fact, I think they are *brilliant*." Sherlock declared. I raised my head again and watched as Sherlock peeled away a sideburn from his cheek, followed by a moustache and finally the facial hair around his eyebrows and chin. I recognised the soft backs of stage makeup and my breath caught in my throat as Sherlock Holmes dumped it all on the table between us.

She leaned back and rubbed the patches on her face where the fake hair had sat. Sighing, she ran her hands through her hair. Those piercing grey eyes shone with mischief as Sherlock propped her legs over the corner of the armchair and crossed them like a lazy feline.

"Apologises for the deception, dear Watson," she said without any sincerity at all. "I couldn't resist."

Suddenly the stupor I had found myself in lifted. I clasped shut my jaw which had fallen during the spectacle, guiding my hands to my head. I had thought myself to be quite perceptive, yet Holmes had made a complete mockery of that.

"You're a *woman*?" I managed to draw out, to which Holmes gestured to herself and then yawned. Had she been waiting for me to wake up?

"That is what biology would say," she said with a quiet, pleasant smile as if she were sharing a private joke with herself. "But alas, my work must be done – and women scare men in this age. Especially those with minds of their own."

How could I have overlooked it so easily? Sherlock went from a refined gentleman to a gentile woman in a blink. And she was beautiful as both. I shed the facial hair, putting it on the table next to hers. I felt my face flush – this was the first time in however many years it had been that another soul, besides myself and God, had seen me out of costume.

Those eyes seemed ever watchful. A nervousness fluttered in my chest like a butterfly taking flight.

"By George, you are a *woman,* aren't you?" Sherlock said, teasing me again. It only made my cheeks burn more.

"As are you, Holmes. If I can even call you that." I crossed my arms.

Holmes was remarkably unfazed by everything that had occurred. It seemed she had already thought through this entire scene. I envied that calmness. My mind was running faster than a steam engine and yet there she was, serene as a lake.

"As you should, as that is my name," she announced, swinging her legs back round to the floor.

"Sherlock is a girl's name?" I asked. To which she shook her shoulders.

"Certainly." She remarked with certainty. "I daresay that John is not, Watson?"

I leaned back into my seat. A weight felt like it had been lifted from my chest; there was someone else like me. She was peculiar and strange, but she seemed like a friend – how odd. Perhaps this was why I regarded her so strangely before, maybe part of me knew. My worries seemed to have eased on her smile – her eyes, though still shining silver, made me relax. Like there was nothing to be fearful of. She had revealed herself first, after all. She was trusting me as much as I was trusting her.

I shook my head, "Watson is my family name. Johanna is my Christian name."

Sherlock nodded.

"I thought as much," she said, resuming her tea with as much ease as if we had just been discussing the weather. "When changing one's identity, people tend to pick names similar to their own. I had guessed Johanna, Josephine, or maybe even Jocelyn."

My own hands were shaking far too much to pick up my tea and join her.

"How do you know all this?" I pressed. "Since I have been John, no one had even guessed at my true identity." There have been a few mishaps with the moustache, or sideburns maybe, in the early days before I bound my chest, but as I'd grown used to the daily application of my makeup, those mishaps had ceased.

Sherlock spoke incredulously. "Well, dear, those people were not me," she said as if that explained everything. I gawped at her.

"You should take your chest binder off too, Watson," Sherlock said with narrowed eyes. "I can't imagine that it is comfortable."

I laughed. I couldn't fathom what I was hearing; my ears were ringing and it felt like I was about to explode.

"It's like being in a corkscrew," I told her. She grimaced.

"It is times like these that I thank my genetics for being as flat as a broadsheet," she said.

"You didn't answer my question. How did you guess?" I asked again. Sherlock rubbed her temples briefly before sighing – as if she were making me privy to some secret treasure.

"I didn't guess, Watson," she said. "Did Stamford tell you of my profession?"

I shook my head.

"I am a consulting detective," she declared. "I solve puzzles, figure out scenes. Every now and then I help the mediocre fellows at Scotland Yard." I could only stare at her. "I am able to make quick deductions about people that lead me to the truth about them – that way I can understand a scene more clearly."

"A detective makes sense," I replied. An investigator – no wonder I was so bridled.

"Consulting Detective," Sherlock corrected me. I gave her a straight look. "Detective makes me think of Lestrade and Gibson at the Yard... Then it makes me feel sad."

I scoffed at that as she smiled. Arrogance and confidence were embodied in her.

"I think I understand you more now," I said to her, "yet you're quite the odd one, Sherlock." I took my cup from its saucer.

She raised her teacup to meet mine. "As are you, John."

The Poisoned Lily

You may have read this tale in the papers before. It stayed in the news for quite some time, and it remains popular with those who follow our adventures in the news. Yet, as is the custom for fanatics, elements have been missed out or exaggerated. However, here I will tell you the breadth of this tale and how poison was at the centre of it.

Poison fascinated my roommate and companion. Our cupboards were full of corked bottles of all kinds of terrible and deadly science. One may, in fact, when looking for a brandy to calm her nerves stumble upon a bottle of cyanide sat beside a box of cigars and mistake it for gin. Had Sherlock not been in the kitchenette too, I would have surely met my fate that very evening. She had laughed herself hoarse.

"You should've left a note!" I exclaimed as Sherlock very carefully funnelled the liquid back into its bottle. She popped the cork back in, her shoulders still shaking with silent giggles.

"I didn't think you would be so foolish as to pour a liquid that clearly was not labelled for consumption, Doctor," she said amusedly.

It was the eighteenth day of October – a Tuesday – and Sherlock and I were finishing off our breakfast at the table before taking our places by the fire. I had been living with her for a few weeks now, but today something new was afoot.

She was dressed in a pair of straight light trousers with a double-breasted waistcoat tight around her slim waist. There was a black frock coat and scarf hanging near the door, too, that made me curious as to her plans for the day.

"I say, Watson," she said crossing an ankle over her knee. "I am becoming concerned. Was the cyanide an omen for things to come?" A smirk graced the corner of her lips. "I assure you, though London can be a dreary city in the winter months, it gets easier with time."

I shook my head and sipped my tea.

"Please label the poisons from now on," I said with a sigh. "If I am to depart this world, I would desire to go in a more remarkable way than out of sheer carelessness."

Sherlock chuckled to herself. "Consider me wounded, *Sir*. I shall endeavour to remember."

She suddenly stood up and disappeared to her rooms for a few moments before returning with her disguise effortlessly applied to her face – the masculine countenance never failed to astound me.

"I know what will cheer you up, Watson," she said, placing her hands on her hips. "I have opened my services up to the public once more. I am to be accepting cases and clients with all their problems that only I can solve." She puffed up her chest, her gaze settling on me with feverish intensity. "And you are to accompany me."

"Pardon?" I exclaimed. "Holmes, I don't think that is wise."

"Come now," she declared rubbing her hands together. "Don't you long for adventure?"

Truthfully, my eyes had long become too accustomed to the inside of Baker Street. But I also had never had a companion such as her before.

"What if we were caught?" I asked. Holmes raised an eyebrow, looking handsomely incredulous at me. "And the police found out about us?"

"No one would believe them," she said with certainty, adjusting her dark tie at her neck in the mirror above the mantle. She stopped moving and turned to me. I placed my tea down. "Would you?"

"Of course not. But that doesn't stop someone thinking otherwise."

She tutted her tongue on the roof of her mouth.

"Have no fear, Watson," she said slowly. "I can read people like they are broadsheets – if there is any danger, we shall quell any suspicions with an extraordinary display of manliness."

I shot her a glare. "How would you propose we do that?"

She shook her shoulders.

"Be right about everything even when I am wrong. Talk at women instead of to them. Never show emotion even if your leg fell off and floated to York. And, of course, sit on public transport as widely as possible." She said all of this with a serene face.

"That sounds like my Father," I replied bitterly. She laughed.

"I used my brother, Mycroft, as an example," she added. "Loathsomely dull cockroach that he is."

She could not be persuaded out of it. I was to come on her adventures. Sherlock's first row of appointments started at noon, so I was quick to dress in my three-piece grey suit, with a dark tie at my neck.

Sherlock's excitement could not be contained. She pulled out her violin as I was changing and played a merry tune. This went on until I came to sit in our living quarters. That was when we heard our first knock at the door. Mrs Hudson opened the door; she was wearing her usual brown and black striped dress with a soft folded collar. Her bright eyes glowed warmly at the pair of us.

"*Gentlemen*," she declared with a private smile. "Mr Argus Ball."

The first gentleman was a stout fellow past forty, with a mop of brown hair, rounded face, and a tweed flat cap crushed in his palm. He pressed his lips together before speaking in a gruff voice.

"Good Afternoon, sirs. May I presume one of you is Mr Sherlock Holmes?" he asked, still lingering in the doorway like he was debating whether he ought to stay or flee. My friend rose from her seat and stepped forward, grasping the man's hand tightly. He stiffed up instantly as she briskly shook it.

"That would be I, Mr Ball," she said. "Please, take a seat."

His muddy brown eyes flicked over to me as I awkwardly got to my feet. I wondered if I should shake his hand as well.

Noticing this, Sherlock added, "This is my companion, Doctor John Watson. Do you mind him listening in on your problem? He is rather quick when it comes to puzzles and may be of some use."

I glared at her after that description, but her expression didn't change.

Mr Ball switched his curious eyes back to Sherlock. "Certainly," he said lowering his head to me. "Sir."

Sherlock had already turned our chairs at an angle, facing Mr Ball. She offered him tea from the tray that Mrs Hudson had so kindly brought up. He refused politely.

"How may we be of assistance, Mr Ball?" Sherlock said, stretching languidly in her chair, but propped forward to listen. "Please, spare us no details."

I pressed my palms together on my lap. Mr Ball's own hands had still not unwound from his flat cap. He glanced down at the floor, he rubbed his face where his facial hair gathered at his chin and under his nose. A nervous gesture I recognised from my practicing days.

"Right," he started, "my problem is a curious one, indeed. I went to the police, you see, but they could make no sense of any of it. One of the detectives there told me to come to you – rather begrudgingly, I may add."

"Lestrade," Sherlock said to me with a knowingly look. "Scotland Yard. My favourite collection of sillies."

"Pardon, sir?"

"I have curious friends among the bobbies," she said, waving a hand. "Please, continue."

"Yes. You see, I am the owner of a small bakery in Clapham, in the town centre with the rest of the shops. It's called Harvest Breads."

I had been to Clapham many times, myself, and could easily picture the brown and orange bricks that made up the houses there. The roads he spoke of were constantly trodden with the hooves of London traffic.

"It was market day two Saturdays ago," he continued, rubbing his moustache again. "My daughter, Mary, was helping me prepare the morning bread when she noticed this small cart outside our shop, next to the Butcher's. It was painted a bright green, covered in sketches of delicate flowers," he spoke slowly. "Mary, she is my eldest. Has always been by my side since her mother died in the Spring, three years ago. For as long as she's been alive, she's loved flowers. When she saw the cart, she exclaimed in joy and went to the door in her floury apron. There was an older woman dressed in a dark shawl covering her head and hair. She was in a black mourning dress and pushed the cart very slowly up and down the road.

"Of course, my dear Mary was beside herself. She's always at that florist on her days off, bringing back the best flowers for our house – as her mother did before she passed over. So, naturally, I went at lunch to the lady to purchase some for Mary. All the brilliant blooms she had were so bright and festive. Roses in bloom. Wild daisies. Chrysanthemums, bigger than your hand. But the true gem of this cart was a bouquet of orange lilies – glowing like a paraffin lamp, almost as if they had been painted.

"The lady had a deeply wrinkled face, but it was hidden in shadow," he continued. "I was sure I hadn't seen her around before. She said that she was happy to sell them to me and urged me to sniff them straight away."

Mr Ball shook his head there.

"Of course, I went to sniff them but before I could, my daughter Mary came over and took them from me. The old lady gasped – I was very sure it was a gasp, even though she tried to conceal it with a cough. She left with the cart before I could even thank her."

"But that only was the start of it," he exclaimed after a short pause. "Mary started to cough. She contracted quite a fever. We had to call the doctor who informed us that she's had an allergic reaction to the lilies. But, see, she's never had that reaction before. They're her favourite flowers!"

Mr Ball shook his head and clenched his fist.

"She's been bed-ridden for a week now! The lilies must've been poisoned," he proclaimed with surety. I turned to my companion who had folded her hands over in her lap and was tapping her thumbs absent-mindedly.

"You are aware that allergic reactions can be brought on at any point in one's life?" She glanced my way. "Correct, Doctor?"

I nodded once. "Correct as ever, Holmes."

The gentleman gave me a hard look and flapped a hand. He struggled to form the words, making a strangled noise.

"This is no reaction I have ever seen, gentlemen." His face was reddening by the moment. "An hour after the incident, my Mary fell asleep and has not risen since."

"And the woman who sold you the flowers – the one with the cart?" Holmes inquired, her sharp eyes ever watchful, ever knowing.

"Disappeared!" the man exclaimed. "Gone as if she'd never existed. No one has seen or heard her since."

Sherlock processed this with a quick smile and brushed down her trousers with her hands as she stood up. "I think it's about time you take us to your dear daughter, Mr Ball."

After we had finished our other appointments – some of which later blossomed into intriguing cases on their own – we took a taxi to the circuit in Clapham where Harvest Breads lay. The town was as bustling and busy as ever. The streets were full of merchants selling wares and the London air here seemed to smell distinctly of fresh mud, metal machinery, and hot oil.

Yet this small bakery flooded its measly industrial square with the scent of yeast, bread, and sweet pastries. The banner above had been painted in a vibrant bold red, perhaps recently given a new coating.

Much like the bright sign, Sherlock's finely tailored suit made her stand out from the many shades of brick. We cornered many a strange look as we stood outside the bakery.

Mr Ball threw a hand wide at the closed shop – an orange glow grew from inside the place that suggested someone was indeed inside.

"This is my enterprise, gentlemen," he looked nervously to Sherlock, who hadn't spoken during the entire journey – only once when she went to pay the driver. Ball stepped forward and pushed the door wide open.

The smell of yeast and fresh bread enveloped me as if it were a warm embrace. I breathed in deeply, filling my lungs with the enticing aroma. Sherlock glanced my way, giving me a small smile. I felt a red tinge on my cheeks.

A shorter man with dark hair stepped out from behind the counter. He came to about five foot seven in height with a rounded expression, a Roman nose, and bright blue eyes. He sported a floured apron and I took note of the wrinkles in his palms that were filled with white.

"Robert! I didn't know you would be working today," Mr Ball exclaimed. "This is Robert Howard, my apprentice. Bobby, this is Mr Sherlock Holmes and his friend, Doctor Watson."

The boy, who looked to be around nineteen, gazed at Sherlock and me curiously.

"Pleasure to meet you, gents," he said, lowering his head our way. We returned the gesture.

"They're going to puzzle out what happened to our Mary," Mr Ball said, rubbing his hands together nervously. Bobby had immediately perked up at the mention of the Ball daughter, yet, as he realised our role here, his expression dropped.

"So, it *was* poison?" Bobby's nostrils flared and he stared the pair of us down. Mr Ball seemed taken aback. "I can't believe it. Not *our* Mary, good as gold she is, I tell you. Who would dare poison her?"

Sherlock raised a gloved hand at the flaring temper of the boy.

"Let's not jump to conclusions before we have examined all evidence," she said placing her hand back on the top of her cane. She spoke gently but firmly before turning to me, beckoning.

"I think it is about time I see the girl," I told Mr Ball, who was still recovering from his apprentice's outburst. He immediately snapped out of it.

"Certainly, Doctor," he said, casting another look at Bobby. The boy's expression was rigid, his shoulders squared. Our presence had clearly alerted him to the very real possibility of foul play. Mr Ball seemed to be convinced so, anyway.

Mr Ball lead us through to the back into a moderately sized living space and a table in the centre of the room. Plates lay stacked on every surface – no doubt Mary had taken on the housekeeping as her role since her mother's passing. He led us up some wooden stairs that led to a bare hallway and stopped at the first door. Opening it quietly, he tapped gently.

"Mary, love. I've brought a doctor in to see you," he said. The room had the windows flung open wide and light was streaming in. Mary's laboured breaths filled the space – the squeezing and coughing reminded me of the tents I was confined to during the spell of fever when I was abroad. A shiver passed down my back.

I examined the girl closely. Her dark hair lay matted at the base of her skull, the skin around her neck engorged with a cruel rash of hives. There was a fever burning at her cheeks and when her eyes flickered open for a moment, I saw they were tinged red. There was no doubt in my mind that an affliction this strong was an allergic reaction, yet a violent response like this was highly unlikely. I relayed this to Sherlock and Mr Ball looked pleased with validation.

"Mr Ball, could you please describe the flowers once more? Unless you have them to hand?" Sherlock proposed. Mr Ball shook his head.

"Sorry, sir, but I burned them as I suspected them of being the cause of Mary's harm," he said. "They were a bright orange with a lovely dark core at petals' centre."

"Did you notice anything strange about the centre of the lilies? Where the pistil – the long tube-like growths live in lilies?" Sherlock said, tilting her head to the side.

Mr Ball rubbed his head, "Actually, I don't think there were any long middle bits." His forehead wrinkled I thought. "The centre had been cut and was covered in dark pollen."

"It appears to me like the lily was a hoax to draw you in. The pollen was, in fact, a poison meant to be inhaled," Sherlock stated. "By this reaction, I would assume something highly toxic – perhaps foxgloves, dried and crushed before being applied to the lilies."

37

"Why not a chemical poison?" I questioned. "Surely its application would be easier than that."

Sherlock shook her shoulders.

"Indeed, but it is far easier to acquire poison in one's garden than to purchase it – especially if you know what you are looking for."

"What are you suggesting, Holmes?" I said, frustrated. Sherlock looked decidedly smug.

"I think I know where to look for our next lead," she said, strolling out the room, Mr Ball and I barely on her tailcoat. Without turning to us, she tossed, "Among the flowers, of course."

Sherlock had a bewildered Mr Ball point us in the direction of Mary's favourite florist, located a few roads away on Elmhurst Street. We walked briskly – at least, Sherlock did. I could barely catch up.

"Dear Watson, you must learn to quicken your pace. How will we ever get anywhere?" she drawled out after a moment, waiting for me at the end of a road as I scuttled down.

"It is not my fault you are sprinting," I exclaimed, my breathing laboured. "My legs are a great deal shorter than yours."

"Perhaps next time I'll bring a wheelbarrow for you," she added with a smirk as we turned a corner. Thankfully, she slowed her pace a little – just enough for me to keep up with her strides.

After a moment of silence between us, I could hold it in no longer.

"May I ask you a question?" I said. The corner of Sherlock's smile twitched into a grin.

"What a fun paradox," she said to me. "Proceed."

"Holmes, I cannot shake the feeling you have already solved this case." We crossed a road together, minding all the traffic that passed.

"Firstly, that is not a question," she replied, slowing her pace some more. "Secondly, I would have said so if I had already solved it. I have my suspicions and my deductions – but that is all." She suddenly halted her steps and looked at me. "Thirdly," she began before she took her tall hat off for a moment and readjusted her hair before replacing it with a flourish. "We're here."

I looked forward and saw a courtyard of flowers. I hadn't even noticed that we'd drawn so near it. A wired sign spelling out 'Penny's' hung above the yard where ladies in bundles of cotton and wool milled about, serving customers petunias, roses, lilies, and all kinds of flowers of all shapes and sizes. I stepped forward and approached the young seller closest to us. She was wearing a dark flat cap with a few rosebuds pinned on its sides. Her apron was double tied, the pocket jingling with pennies, crowns, and shillings.

"Excuse me, Ma'am." Her doe brown eyes looked up at me. Her face lit up in delight.

"Ma'am!" she cackled and placed a hand on her hip. "I can't remember the last time someone called me ma'am. Now I feel like a real *lady*." She laughed heartily again. A few individuals turned to look our way. I felt my face flush stupidly. I didn't need to look at Holmes to know she was chuckling, too. "What can I do for you, gentlemen? I have two peonies for a shilling or six for two."

"We are looking for a young man in your employment. Tall with red or fair hair?" Sherlock said stepping forward. "We need to talk to him about a case we are working concerning the baker's daughter – Mary Ball."

I shot daggers at Holmes she smiled as innocent as a lamb.

"How did you come to that description?" I hissed her way. The description had been a short lady with a dark shawl covering her features.

"It's elementary, my dear Watson. Anyone with unremarkable features will go for a less daring disguise. Thus I can only assume that our gentleman had some remarkable features, such as fair hair or a red shade that stands out among his peers. As for the height, one can only deduce that appearing hunched over was to add to this rouse of appearing old and senile."

The girl in front of us thought for a moment, pressing a finger onto her chin and tapping it once.

"Perhaps you mean our Eddie," she said after a beat. "I'm afraid he's been unwell recently, contracted the flu. I assume he'll be in bed."

Sherlock nodded.

"Indeed," she tapped her cane once. "This is a matter of some urgency, I'm afraid. Could you please give us his address?"

The girl skittered off to bring her boss. From her, we learned he lived in Cedar Mews, behind the church, in an apartment he rented from them.

Before we set off, Sherlock, ever the charmer, bought a pair of violet posies from the girl who introduced herself as Eliza. Sherlock tucked one of the violets in my coat's chest pocket before I could protest.

"To match your cheeks," she said before practically skipping away from my scowling face.

"Unnecessary," I called after her figure speeding on in front of me.

"This better not become a regular outing, Holmes," I said. "I wish to practice medicine again at some point. "I told her as the church came into view. We followed the path around the back. Sherlock stopped and we both clapped eyes on a barrow full of dirt where flowers sprung from it.

More dirt lay around it. Clearly, it had been hastily filled up with soil as the flowers sat fresh in their beds.

"So, this boy wanted to cause the girl harm," I tried to assemble the scene in my mind. "What was his motive? A broken heart, perhaps?"

"That is what I thought as well," Sherlock said and I was quite impressed with myself for a moment. "Then I thought why would he attack the girl? The heart is a fickle thing but an intense thing when it knows what it wants." She ground her teeth together before her eyes lit up. "It wasn't meant for her at all."

Of course, she had already figured out what had just dawned on me.

"Mr Ball!" I concluded as we arrived at the apartment. The church had been left in a state of disarray; this place was no better. "If he was out of the way, our man would have an easier time introducing himself to her."

"Almost." Sherlock rapped her knuckles on the door.

A red-haired young man greeted up. He had a healing black eye and what looked to be a broken nose. Clearly, something had gone awry.

"Good afternoon, sir," Sherlock said extending a hand. "We are investigating a case concerning one Miss Mary Ball. We would like to ask you some questions."

The young man's dark eyes darted between the pair of us before lunging forward, shoving us apart and making his way through the garden.

"Oh, charming," Sherlock was already making chase. I ran after them, but it wasn't long before my chest started burning. Sherlock was quicker than a barrel from a gun. She soon had that boy, tripping him forward with her cane. He fell to the floor and the knock to his head rendered him dazed. We carried him back to the bakery and called the Yard to come and collect him.

Mr Ball was inconsolable when he saw us drag Eddie into the bakery.

"You?!" he yelled at the top of his lungs. "I'll make garters from your guts!"

He raged forward and it took both Sherlock and I to hold him back. Bobby took hold of the red-headed boy. The stone look on his face stilled Eddie's struggling.

"Sir! Get a hold of yourself!" Sherlock called after putting some space between them. "The Yard will see justice done."

"You monster!" Mr Ball cried. "You poisoned my girl! After you had the audacity to ask for her hand!"

Eddie's face fell bitterly. Sherlock took a deep breath and cleared her throat.

"The poison was actually meant for you."

Mr Ball spluttered a response. Everything fell in place in my mind.

"After Eddie had grown fond of Mary's visiting the florists, naturally he asked you for permission to court her," she explained. "However, Mary did not feel the same way and had you refuse him. This did not go down well as you can see by young Eddie's face."

"So, Eddie planned your demise with a disguise and some flowers which he knew were her favourite," she continued. "Only she came over herself. Eddie didn't want to expose himself, so he allowed her to smell the blooms, thus, poisoning her."

For a moment, there was silence in the bakery. Sherlock flicked a speck of lint away from her jacket as she looked between the men.

"I believe that is correct, is it not?" she looked to Eddie. His silence confirmed it.

"Bloody Henry," Mr Ball exclaimed. "How did you know about that? I told no one."

Sherlock shrugged her shoulders. " Once I saw your apprentice's affection for your daughter, I knew her heart belonged to another. A look at Eddie's face confirmed it," she explained. "How long have you two been engaged?"

Bobby's jaw dropped and he scratched his head, looking bashful. "A month," he said.

Sherlock nodded, "I see."

"You're engaged?" Mr Ball's face was the picture of
surprise and he yelled loud enough the windows shook.

The Coven of Fleet Street

This story is not a well-known one, for it dabbles in the superstition of curious minds. Naturally, it is one of Sherlock's favourites.

"It is always a pleasant day when you wake up to find none of your past relatives lounging in your flat, dear Watson," Sherlock said, she was sprawled out longwise across her seat. "The veil has closed and the dead have passed beyond." She was wearing only a thin nightgown. The morning light hung around her head like a halo, dark hair sprawled across her fair face.

The first day of November was a chill one, the fire already lit and glowing. Yet her face was pale. I felt suddenly as if I was overdressed in my outfit, but Sherlock had instructed to be ready by noon.

Glancing over my outfit, a twinge of a smile graced her lips, her eyebrow-raising upward as if pulled by a string.

"So formal," she remarked. "Are we going somewhere?"
I could smell it then. Hot embers from burning opium. There was a pipe next to her seat that I hadn't seen until now. It was already done with, of course.

Sherlock was careful enough to not engage in the activity around me, knowing I would scold her. Her smile turned more angelic by the moment. The slender features and grey eyes that always looked sharp were softening.

"We have appointments, Holmes," I said, lowering my body onto my own seat. Her gaze made the hair on the back of my neck rise. I helped myself to some tea that was already waiting on the table.

Sherlock puffed a sigh.

"Do we really?" she said, examining the lines of her cuticles before closing her eyes.

"Yes, Holmes," I replied. She didn't move – perhaps she was in a mood about something. Her gaze seemed distant. There were frown lines etching on her forehead. "Any reason for the dour mood?" Her previously relaxed jaw snapped shut.

"Have Mrs Hudson tell them to come back tomorrow," she said suddenly, kicking her legs over the seat. Sherlock stood up slowly, using her usual languidness. "It is time for you to meet my favourite brother."

The Diogenes Club was a townhouse off of Carlton House Terrace. I noticed as we walked up that everything was kept most orderly. Sherlock's bitter mood was not to be shaken today – nothing I said could sway her. She had picked a tailored three-piece suit in black for the occasion, along with a long woollen coat with a military chest of bronze buttons.

Next to her, I felt like a weed sprung from a crack in the pavement wearing my usual tweed and flat-cap. I silently scorned the detective for not warning me of the improperness of my dress.

The door to the building had a sign welded to its door. The handle looked as if it had been newly repaired.

'*Gentlemen's Club: No Women*' shone on a bronze plaque next to the door. Usually, Sherlock would've made a joke about such a sign. *Women invading the privacy of men, whatever next? Votes?* But her steely countenance today showed no such approval of breaking trivial sexisms as these.

"I do apologise, my dear," she said in a low voice as we stepped into a square room with a marble floor. Sprawling out around us were seating arrangements with sofas and chaise lounges made of green velvet. Gentlemen ranging from the old and grey to the young and keen were engaged in various degrees of chatter around dishes laden with cakes and delicate cups of tea. Sherlock stepped keenly forward, and I noticed many a head rise to peer at us. She ignored the lull in conversation, but I kept my gaze either up or at the floor. Ahead of us was a receptionist. He sat behind a great oaken desk. The gentleman had ebony skin and was wearing a suit of fine quality. He lowered his head respectfully. "This place is most tedious."

"Mr Holmes," the receptionist greeted her, getting to his feet. He wore a burgundy satin waistcoat adorned with golden buttons. His hair was cut short and parted at the side. The man extended a white glove, indicating to our left. Sherlock did not say anything. "Mr Holmes has been inspecting you in the Chapel rooms," the gentleman continued. "If you would follow me."

Sherlock steamed onwards, leaving me behind feeling mortified. However, the gentleman did not look surprised by this rudeness, in fact, he tilted his head to me. "It seems the young master knows where he is going." He gave me a graceful smile before returning behind the desk.

"Apologies, for my companion, sir," I said quickly, scurrying past him. "He's sat under a dark cloud today."

I caught up with Sherlock and nudged her in the arm, successfully bringing her attention to me. Her face was framed in such a moment of rage that my heart shuddered. Yet upon realising it was only me, she quickly relaxed.

"What was that behaviour, Holmes?" I hissed at her. She scoffed.

"He has had worse from me," she said bitterly. "Never fear, I always apologise on the way out."

Suddenly we arrived at a tall mahogany door with the words Chapel emblazoned on in gold. She flung it open with such a force that it ricocheted against the wall and needed to be forced away as Sherlock swanned in. I quickly followed before the door could slam shut behind me. My horrification appeared to have no end as my companion jumped over a chaise lounge and claimed a giant armchair near the roaring fire.

A prim male voice spoke then broke me out of my inner fire of despair.

"It is nice to see you, too, Sherlock," called from the window. I looked up from my sulking companion to see a gentleman clasping a pipe by the window, breathing smoke through a thick red moustache. He wore a charcoal grey suit with a black waistcoat and tie. The gentleman carried a silver-topped cane-like Sherlock's, but his had an ergonomic shape on top rather than a fox. His hair was thinner than Sherlock's, but it framed his face nicely nonetheless. Mycroft Holmes must've been in his mid-thirties and aside from his sturdier stature that was in sharp contrast with Sherlock's leanness, he was a rather handsome man.

Clearly, beauty ran in their family – unlike in mine where my brother had absorbed all the good genetics, leaving me as plain as flour.

"Mycroft. "Sherlock said with a nod as a way of greeting. She sat with her legs splayed and, to my surprise, pulled a cigar from her coat pocket. She lit it before speaking again. "How is life for you going, being the only semblance of competence in the whole ruling government?"

I perched on the chaise next to her and crossed my ankles. Mycroft's gaze fell on me, his eyes narrowed like he was unsure of what to make of me. As he turned back to Sherlock his mouth twisted into a sneer.

"Can't you at least sit like a lady?" he said exasperatedly. "Mother would be spinning in her grave."

Sherlock took a deep breath in and blew rings of smoke out. I kept my face as still as possible as she hooked a leg over each arm of the chair. Her back was halfway down the seat and she couldn't have possibly been comfortable.

"Better?" she said before another long drawl.

Mycroft rolled his eyes.

"Doctor John Watson, I presume?" he said looking at me intently before extending a hand. I got to my feet and took it.

"Pleasure to meet you, sir," I replied. I could feel Sherlock looking daggers into the back of my head at the betrayal I would no doubt be ranted at for later.
"I was curious to meet a man of your standing having found companionship in our waylaid Sherlock," he added. There was a ghost of a smirk on his lips. "Now I understand why, *ma'am.*"

My heart dropped to my shoes.

"Don't go frightening her away, Mycroft," Sherlock barked while trying to sit upright, but her own position was proving an obstacle. "Just because you prefer total solitude does not mean I have to."

Mycroft only huffed a sigh before taking the seat opposite us. He glanced at me once more, his lips pressed firmly together as if he didn't know what to make of me. Then he offered me a full smile.

"Companionships worth keeping are rare to come by, Sherlock," he said sharply. "My own company is far more intimate. I have a job for you."
Sherlock clenched her jaw, ensnaring her brother with a glare.

"Why can't you do it?" she said, pointedly sticking her chin in his direction. "Or is it too difficult for your tiny brain?" Mycroft nearly scowled at her then. Perhaps it was my presence that was restraining him from being more forward.

"Nonsense," he said a little too quickly. "I have enough cases. However, given *your* advertisement in the Telegraph, I believed that you were down on your luck and this case would be better suited in a *woman's* hands."

I knew a storm was about to hit. I leaned back in my seat as Sherlock unhooked her legs and leaned forward, ready to fight. Unfortunately, this just seemed to fire up Mycroft even more.

"Oh, so it involves women then," she said, baring her teeth. Her lips formed a pantomime smile, contorting her face into that of a theatre mask. "No wonder you're clueless behind needed assistance." Mycroft's glare was so sharp, its edges could easily cut us in half. Sherlock continued, "Have no fear – my experience there makes yours look pitifully sad and… Disappointing."

Mycroft abruptly got to his feet, the chair scraping against the sudden friction, and stalked back to the window.

"When you are finished behaving like an infant in front of your new partner, the file is on the table," he said slapping it down. "Message my office in Westminster." He lowered his head to me quickly before leaving, "Goodbye, Doctor – pleasant meeting you."

I heard his feet retreating down the hall and a door slam shut. I looked back to Sherlock, whose grin was maniacal. She began to laugh and laugh. When she noticed my stunned expression, she laughed harder.

"Was that necessary?" I exclaimed to her, standing up. "He wanted help!"

Sherlock finally ceased laughing and rubbed a tear away from her eye.

"He didn't really," she said. "Mycroft just wanted a good look at you to confirm his own suspicions. Naturally, I had to make him pay for his own arrogance and pitiful attitude towards females." That hadn't crossed my mind at all but it was the only picture she could see. "Have no fear. That is our usual greeting – he berates me, I berate him back. He can't handle it, and off he goes." Sherlock sighed before slipping off her coat and draping it over the seat. "Tis a yuletide tradition," she added with glee.

She swiped the file off the table and sat on it, a leg pulled up on her right so she could rest her chin on her knee.

"A new case that the mighty Mycroft cannot solve – tricky indeed," she said flipping it open. It took a moment for her to scan over the contents. "This file begins with the statement from one Mr Cartwright – an accountant who occupies offices at Charing Cross. He firstly makes a point emphasizing his clear mental health and sturdy mind before relaying the events of the night before." A small smile appeared on Sherlock's face. "There is even a doctor's signature here! Always good to reassure one's reader of the soundness of one's mind."

"Certainly, when the tale involves women," I replied, "as relayed by men."

Sherlock nodded approvingly. "Indeed."

"Mr Cartwright's tale begins as thus," she cleared her throat and adopted a deeper male tone, sounding eerily similar to her brother's. "I was closing up my office in the early hours of the morning after having completed a taxing workload. However, I had promised my wife a return, so I made tail to our home on Shoe Lane. Having got a taxi to the end of the lane I departed, saving the pennies for the whole fare by walking the final step to the door. However, a strange sensation did overcome me then. A sickness that inflicted my head and made it as light as if full of hot air."

"Oh, goodie," Sherlock said – unperturbed as usual – before reading on, "I was so overcome with this newfound affliction I passed out on the stairs of one of the nearby houses. But not before I saw a great green light appear in the sky and heard a cackle of laughter. The last thing I saw was pointed hats and ladies with great beaks, warts, and dark skin. In the year of our Queen, I would have never thought witchcraft still afoot – yet I have been gravely mistaken. There are witches in London, sir, I assure you. They long for the death of working men such as myself." She paused over the last paragraph. "Alas, I awoke in my own bed, my soiled clothes already washed, dried, and folded."

Sherlock flipped through the remaining lone page which appeared to be the record of the time and date the accountant had delivered his statement. She shut the folder and dropped it onto the table.

"The man is mad?" I asked, the only reasonable explanation to such delusions. Sherlock flopped down into the seat next to me. "After Cartwright has so admirably demonstrated his stable-mindedness? Infallible, Watson."

"I am a doctor, Holmes," I reply, taking the file into my lap. "Bluntness is a courtesy in my trade." It was only those two sheets after all – and a pen's scribble on the back of the statement. *Whitefriars* was written in quick cursive.

"The pen is a curious note," Sherlock remarked as I ran a finger over it. She huffed another sign. "There is no doubt what this is though – a clue, from my royal brother himself."

"Holmes, is not a complicated case something you have been longing for?" I said as she scowled at the wall. "Stop whinging and use your brain."

"Who says I find this complicated?" She raised an eyebrow at me.

"Well, I for one, do," I pursed my lips and closed the folder. "'Tis a mystery. No witnesses. No further information. Just a testimony and a road name."

"You got confused at the Crimson Moustache Gentlemen case. Becoming easily perplexed is a talent of yours," she scoffed. I swatted her with the file. "Fine, fine. I have already drawn some conclusions, but further illumination is required."

We enjoyed a cup of hot brewed, gold-leaf tea alongside some lavender tea biscuits with the daintiest sponge cakes to accompany. I indulged myself while Sherlock pondered over the case.

"Fleet Street, home of the written word," she said, admiring the scalloped edge of her biscuit before taking a bite. "Perhaps the publishing industry has taken occult steps to ensure a profitable business."

"I hardly think witches are the cause of this gentleman's delusions. It appears to be a case of the overactive imagination of a tired gentleman," I declared before finishing the rest of my tea.

"Ah, never rule out any possibilities," Sherlock said.

We gathered out things. I pulled my wallet out and Sherlock shook her head.

"The Diogenes Club is headed by my brother – he will fit the bill." Then she swanned out ahead of me before I could retort.

Fleet Street was a bustle of wagons and carriages; newsboys stood flogging papers to those passing. It was a riotous site of men from all walks of life, bustling in offices or on the pavements before the towering buildings that cast legacy shadows on those that walked beneath.

"Smell that air, Watson," Sherlock said grandly, tapping her walking stick on the ground as she strolled on, bobbing and weaving through the foot traffic as the true

Londoner she was. "Ink. Oil. Sweat. These printing presses smell like life."

All I could smell was the burning coal used to make the machines run or the steaming engines of carriages rushing past. The mud they churned up underfoot mixed with rainwater and horse waste.

"In that case, life reeks."

Sherlock paused at the corner and offered me a smile.

"Unfortunate that our witches reside on one of the busiest rows in London," I add, recalling the testimony. My companion pursed her lips, gripping the top of her cane.

"An astute observation, Watson. I daresay we should return here later. This case seems to require an early morning trip."

I grumbled the next morning when Sherlock rapped on my door– early mornings were never my strongest suit. Sherlock disregarded my colourful words as she usually did when it came to "quibbles" such as these. She made me a sugary tea to wake me up and rattled off her notes from the day before. I went with her into the brisk morning air, knowing well that if I did not go willingly – she would drag me.

We headed to do an inspection of Whitefriars Road too which was the clue given to us from Mycroft. The side alley was a shadow compared to the bustle of Fleet Street. The houses were just as high, yet the only occupants were an artisanal brewery and several residential properties. Flowers spilled out of their boxes and under windowsills. The smell of lavender and thyme from a kitchen filled the air with a floral scent that was a far cry from the scent of the dirt on the street. Nothing untoward in sight, only beauty, and neatness.

"Look here, Watson." Sherlock had stopped at the end of the street. A townhouse stood before her, the plaque on it reading *St Margaret's House: Boarding Available.*

"Maybe they saw something?" I wondered. Sherlock seemed to wonder that as well. She knocked on the door briskly. A short, fair maid came to the door. We enquired for the Mistress or Master of the house.

"Lady Everton is out visiting family, I am afraid, sirs," she said. Sherlock left a note with the maid and promised to call on another day. However, before we fully moved from the area, she raised her eyebrows at the door, sniffing the air.

"Can you smell that?" she asked. "The slight metal tinge."

I inhaled deeply. Surely enough, the barest hint of metal hit my senses.

"What is it?" I pondered. "Iron?"

Sherlock shook her head, "Nitrous Oxide. Good to see the note on identifying chemical odour I wrote the other day for the paper has come in handy after all."

"I would've missed it. London is forever a barrel of smells and most of them are most foul."

Sherlock grinned – self-satisfied but kept her retort to herself.

"Come along, Watson. Back to Baker Street, we go. We shall return under the cloak of night. There's still a mystery to solve." She tapped my head once with her cane.

We returned and Sherlock didn't speak to me for a great few hours. She took up companionship with her pipe. Soon our flat filled with puffs of grey smoke. She only did this whenever she was deep in thought, mulling over whatever and everything else.

As midnight edged towards us, I felt tiredness tug at my eyes. Sherlock, however, was wide-awake, sat in her coat and hat, pipe still in her mouth. The glow of the hearth lit her face up and the greys in her eyes burned in thought.

Whenever I offered her tea she only shook her head. Mrs Hudson brought us trays of dinner, despite my request that we could cook for ourselves; but Sherlock did not touch it. After I had finished the meal of mutton and vegetables and returned the plate I sat opposite Sherlock and watched her eyes, glazed over as they were, staring into the fireplace.

I realised I had been staring when Sherlock turned her gaze on me. The corner of her lips twitched into a smile.
"Care to share whatever is on your mind, dear Watson?" she asked, looking back to the orange embers of the fire. "Your pressing eyes are unnerving me."

"Only that I understand how your brother needed assistance with this one," I said. Sherlock bristled and crossed her arms.

"I told you, Mycroft just wanted to get under my skin," she said. "If we don't solve it he'll enjoy reminding me how inferior I am to him."

"I feel this case may be a limit for you and I," I admitted. Sherlock frowned at me. "We have no leads, no witnesses, and only one testimony. It's an unbreakable egg."

"Speak for yourself, Watson," Sherlock tutted. Her tone was clipped. I felt my temper flare – this brusque mood had soured mine.

"If you really loathe your brother this much then maybe you should cut ties," I said, placing my hands on my hips. "For it is not worth the bad temperament it puts you in."

Sherlock chuckled then before placing her pipe down. She pressed her hand over mine. It was a very feminine gesture, one that I wasn't expecting. She ran her thumb over my knuckles and to my surprise, my heart fluttered. Her fingers were unexpectedly soft apart from callouses on her fingertips from playing the violin.

"I'm sorry, John," she said quietly. "Mycroft brings out the worst in me." She didn't move her hand away, rather kept it where it sat over mine. "As for the case – I believe I know why my brother gave it to me."

"How so?" I asked.

Sherlock sent a soft smile my way. I couldn't help tensing as held onto me as she got up. Goosebumps shot up my arms. She sent the grandfather clock on the mantel a glance.

"I will show you."

Fleet Street looked deserted in comparison to how it had been earlier. There were a few couples strutting home after their nightly opera of theatre outings. Drunks hanging next to their carriages, ladies in dark satins next to them.

Sherlock had the taxi drop us off by Whitefriars. The smell of burning metal was stronger than ever, but its source in the darkness was all but a mystery.

"Watson, if you wouldn't mind following me?" Holmes lead us up the lane. She walked a long path between two grey brick buildings before stopping in front of a sneaky black gate.

"Of course, you know all the creepiest sites in London," I said as she used her cane to open it up. The metallic smell burned my nostrils as we got closer.

"Of course, I do," Sherlock smirked. We made our descent down. "Truthfully, I wasn't sure about this case until the maid mentioned who owned that boarding house."

The room suddenly opened up into a long thin space with ancient stone making up the walls.

There inside was an array of tables, chairs, and all manner of scientific equipment. Ladies were skirting around the busy site. The moment we stepped in, movement ceased. The women all froze and shared looks of fear between themselves. I put my hands up reflectively while Sherlock simply smiled at them.

"May I talk to Lady Everton, please?" she asked politely. A young lady dressed in a brown frock with black petticoats bobbed a curtsy and scuttled off. I looked up towards the ceiling.

"Is this a crypt?" I was unsure London had a record of any place such as this.

"Yes. But officially, it doesn't exist," was Sherlock's smug reply.

"Sherlock Holmes," a booming voice came from the end of the room – a lady dressed in green cottons swayed forward, her hair bundled high on her head with ribbons. Lady Everton was of middle-age and sported a light pair of spectacles, walking with all the grace of a lady. I bowed to her Ladyship, which rewarded me with a look of amusement.

"None of that here, Sir. We are but one and the same – lovers of the scientific art!" she exclaimed, indicating around the room elegantly with her arms. "Dear Holmes, I never thought we would see you again after Scotland Yard rumbled our little display at Tower Bridge. Have you not received my letters?"

Sherlock smiled. Clearly, it was a tale from before my move to London.

"Well, I am glad to find you found more suitable living quarters," she said, looking about. "I daresay I have not. We reside at 221B Baker Street now. You must visit us for tea."

Lady Everton smiled joyfully at the invitation.

"I shall have my secretary arrange it," she clasped her hands together. "As charming as your surprise visit is, may I inquire after the cause?"
The ladies behind Lady Everyone had resumed their studies. I saw women walking about with clipboards, wearing gloves as they measured chemicals. Those closest to us were somewhat distracted, however, perhaps in hopes to catch a word or two as they listened on.

"A case, your Ladyship." I was finally able to voice something. "John Watson, ma'am. A pleasure."

The Lady bowed her head to me and gave me a debonair smile that made my ears warm.

"Naturally, *men* of the law you both are," she said crossing her gloved hands over. "I do believe this has something to do with an incident from a week ago."

"Ah, so where is Mr Cartwright's maid, then?" Sherlock said.

A young girl of about eighteen years stepped forward. Her blonde hair was tied in two milkmaid braids going over her head. She wore a bashful look on her face.

"I am sure you are aware, sirs," the girl explained quickly, "but any gaseous experiments are done in the back room where the connection to the sewers is strongest so any airborne chemicals may evaporate instantly."

"That was how Mr Cartwright was caught unawares by a combination of chloroform and paraffin – a few inhales without a proper mask renders one quite dizzy and, in severe cases, can make you see some remarkable things," her Ladyship went on to say, a smile tugging at her lips yet again. "Witches, indeed."

Sherlock chuckled lowly.

"Your knowledge of London's Yard never fails to amuse me, my Lady," Holmes replied amusedly. Her Ladyship never faltered.

"One must keep London's bloodhounds at bay, showing them that we are but delicate flowers. Lest we be made *witches*," she said with amusement. "Feel free to stay, gentlemen. Now, if you will excuse me, I have chemistry to teach."

Sherlock didn't need persuasion as she unbuttoned her coat. I followed suit. There was no doubt she had admirers here, given her frequent articles on the subject published in the paper.

"What should we tell your brother?" I asked, adding my own coat to the hangers on the side. There was a great fire in the centre that kept the crypt toasty warm. "This *was* his challenge."

Sherlock grinned at me.

"The man was tired," came her reply as she led me to a table near her ladyship.

"That is all."

The Stolen Rites

This story was recorded by both myself and those at Scotland Yard – yet the account that was published in the papers did evade some of the details that were important at the time of the event. This was a case that happened once upon a December, one that concerned eleven jilted brides and one thing that evaded them all – the groom.

Despite the frosting upon the ground, our apartment at 221B Baker Street was toasty warm. Mrs Hudson had kept our log manger filled with wood, so we read our cases by the stove. Sherlock had found incense that smelled like warm cinnamon and I brewed us winter-spiced tea with a side of stollen – a German cake that had appeared in London's bakeries. My companion was very fond of it and had ordered a few dozen cakes to keep us well supplied into the New Year.

"Holiday traditions are important to me," she declared. "Yuletide is a perfect time to be celebrating with those you care about. It is also the yearly time that I am roped into going to church or have to honour my mother's memory by sending my brother a gift of clementines." The space between her eyebrows pinched in contempt. "Perhaps I should send him a sack of coals, instead."

I had sent my brother a few chosen items from Portobello Road – a cone of honey nuts, a lambswool tartan scarf, and a selection of scenic postcards from London. He was a sentimental man when it came to material things. I knew he would love the gifts.

It was the 23rd of December and London was still throng with business, yet our cases had ceased for the holiday. We were enjoying reading together. Earlier that day, Sherlock played her violin beautifully for me. She played such tuneful melodies with such ease it made me melt into my seat. Or she played melancholic songs that made me shiver. I was honoured she played for me at all – it seemed a private love when I had met her. But now we'd lived together for months we were somewhat inseparable. We even attended a performance in Shakespeare's Globe. However, not that I would inflate her ego anymore, but personally I would prefer her company, sitting in our armchairs by the warmth of the fire than on a cold wooden seat, all despite the small firepit in our theatre box.

"It's Christmas, Holmes," I replied. "Be nice."

"I am always nice," she muttered, her eyebrows raised. I narrowed my eyes at her.
"And I am the Queen of England."

"Oh, your highness," she said, flipping the page of her book. "I didn't realise you were in town."

I sipped my tea, pointedly not looking in her direction.

A knock at the door disturbed the tranquillity that we had built.

"Come in," I called.

Mrs Hudson opened the door gently – her dark hair was swept up into a bun, done up with a delicate pin adorned with silver flowers. Her dress was green, with a plush velvet collar. There was even rouge on her cheeks, I noticed with surprise. Downstairs she was playing music on a gramophone that now drifted up the stairs to us.

"Sorry, my dears," she said popping her head through. "There are some very persistent women at the door for you."

Sherlock sent me a sharp look. I raised my hands.

"I didn't invite anyone!" I said.

"What do they want?" Sherlock demanded, way too invested in her book.
My companion didn't read for the gratification of a fiction tale – rather, she was reading about the various bodily acids used in digestion. A case involving a dismembered stomach had inspired her and she had been addicted to the biology books I'd lent her ever since. She pored over every word, meticulously taking notes.

Mrs Hudson shook her head. "Heaven knows! They only said they would talk to you, Sherlock."

Sherlock frowned, but ultimately her curiosity won over her textbook fixation. She looked once more to me before shutting her book. All I could offer her was a shrug.

"Please sent them up, Mrs Hudson." Mrs Hudson, her cheeks pink from what I assumed was sherry given it being the evening and because she had company.

Quickly, Sherlock and I transformed into our male alter-egos. She just needed to put on her facial hair, but I, myself, took a bit longer in order to bind my chest and apply my own stage makeup. Moments later, we heard high-heeled shoes in the corridor. A light knock at the door followed. Sherlock got to her feet and leaned an elbow against the top of the armchair.

The door pushed open to reveal a lady with blonde hair coiffed into beautiful ringlets on either side of her face. The rest was tied back neatly with a black ribbon. Her delicate cheeks were flushed with effort, but I noted there were deep shadows around her eyes. She couldn't have been more than eighteen years of age.

"Mr Holmes?" she asked stepping through the doorway. A second later another lady of similar age – also blonde, but with a more handsome face and feline eyes stepped into the room behind her. A blue velvet plush was draped around her shoulders and leather gloves, the lady dressed smartly for the evening as well.

"I beg you, please forgive my impertinence for appearing on your doorstep so unexpectedly. But the detective told us you may be able to help," the first lady addressed Sherlock, quickly discovering she was, indeed, the man for the job. The second woman's shoulders had gone rigid. Perhaps she was debating her justification on simply demanding an audience or was simply steeling her resolve.

"Indeed, Miss," Holmes said crossing her arms. "Who may you be?"
"Miss Eliza Bird, sir," she said, pressing her lips together, her hands folded tightly, before dipping into a curtsy. Her companion mirrored the action. "This is Miss Ethel Maynard."

Ethel nodded once towards both of us – her eyes were narrow.

"Pray tell us which of Scotland's debonair bunch sent you?"

"A man called Lestrade," Miss Bird said, sniffing indignantly, "He was quite heartless towards me before then."

"Ah, Lestrade. Very opinionated, quite useless," Sherlock chuckled.

"Please, ladies take a seat," I directed them to the armchairs, throwing Sherlock a pointed glare. "I will prepare some tea."

My companion bared her teeth in a roguish smile. "Start from the beginning, Miss Bird," I heard Holmes say as I found the cooper whistling pot and lit the gas stove. "Spare no detail."

"I shall start when this began in March this year," Eliza inhaled a deep breath and began the story. It was as if she had been carrying her worries inside her chest for quite a while. "My father passed away, leaving me with the care of my younger sister Adelaide. Our mother has been dead a long time, you see, since we were both very young. Our house is on Smith Terrace; my father had hoped that I would inherit it… Yet, when the bronchitis took him, the government decreed I wasn't allowed to own it legally. That I must marry or else my home would go to my cousin." Her face grew hard. Her companion sat in silence and listened; face was just as stony.

"But I have never had luck with men," she cried. "I cannot seem to find one who would have suitable interest in a future with me. Rather they're all just someone who would have me for today. My father's sickness prevented him from securing a match for either my sister and myself, and I have always been far too busy looking after him and the house to find one on my own."

My heart sank. It must've felt like her problems were weighty indeed. Indeed, if I had not adopted the guise of John, I, too, would have faced similar troubles. Instead, I was a bachelor – a feat acceptable in the eyes of the law. Meanwhile, Miss Bird and her companion did not have the luxury and security of such disguise.

"I am afraid that the law only serves the men who make it," Holmes said as the pot began to whistle on the stove. "Please, don't let me interrupt you."

"That it does," Miss Bird concurred. "I made some enquires through my married friends – a woman of good fortune should be inundated with courtship requests." Her face fell. "Yet, I was not. Instead, people gossiped, spreading rumours of my father's unexpected death. I believed the house to be the main draw that would make me an acceptable match for many, and I was frightfully worried when none sought me." A pause. "Then I met Mr Dartmouth and I fell completely and utterly in love."

I came in and offered tea – both women accepted and Sherlock had another cup too.

"Ah, wonderful," Holmes said, her voice surprisingly stark. "And you came from your wedding party to see me?"

Eliza's eyes shot wide open. "How did you know my wedding party was today?"

"Thank you for your retelling, Miss Bird," Holmes replied instead, sinking into her armchair. "I believe I can grasp the end of the tale myself."

Miss Bird opened her mouth and closed it twice. Her companion, Miss Maynard, simply gawked. Before either of them could speak again, Sherlock finished her sip of tea and leaned back.

"Judging by the delicate lace gloves you have on, as well as the smell of fresh flowers – specifically nosegays and orange blossoms, much like our beloved queen wore when she wed his royal highness – I deduced that either you had come from a wedding or were heading to one. Given the dark shadows under your eyes, I assume not all is well with your suitor, Mr Dartmouth. Let me guess, he procured a dowry from you to pay for the wedding, assured you that this was all in order and correct. But, as you arrived for the ceremony, the wedding had not been arranged and the broom was missing."

Both women stared at her. Sherlock wasn't finished yet, however.

"Judging by your companion's similar state of dress and grim expression, I presume this is no surprise to her. Miss Maynard suffered the same fate as yourself."

"Yes," Miss Maynard spoke up then. "He introduced himself as Mr Daniels to me – but our descriptions match. The wedding was meant to be two days hence, but he never showed." Her face crumpled ad she took a long sip of her tea, a rogue tear sliding down her cheek before it got swiped in haste. "I am in desperate need of the money from the dowry he stole as I cannot afford my mother's medicine without it."

"You're sure that Mr Dartmouth and Mr Daniels are indeed the same man?" I asked. Miss Bird was feverishly nodding her head.

"Yes, because you see, Mr Holmes, you're missing one crucial factor," she turned to Sherlock. "There are eleven of us. Eleven almost-brides."

"This case is quite prolific, Lestrade," Holmes reprimanded the detective as soon as we got to the station. We'd just calmed the young ladies and sent them on their way. Miss Bird had left her address for us to contact her had we any news.

Lestrade sat with his arms crossed, a stern look on his rodent-like face. We knew the detective quite well given our case repertoire together. He did not like being lectured, so naturally, it was Sherlock's favourite thing to do when she was around him.

"Young women have been severely mistreated," I added. "Eleven girls, all jilted by one man – it would be quite the scandal." It would also make a smashing tale if we could solve it and return the money to the women in question.

"Look, Holmes," Lestrade started, giving me a nasty side-eye and ignoring me as he liked to do. "The man in question, if indeed it is one man and not just a tale spun by a string of unlucky ladies, has used a pseudonym. Judging by the conflicting accounts of his facial features and voice, he is indeed very adaptable when it comes to disguises." He crossed his arms assuredly. "This case, if you can even call it that, is dead in the water. There are no leads, no actual evidence aside from the testimonies of a few emotionally-compromised women."

At our unimpressed expressions, Lestrade leaned back and rubbed his whiskery chin with a sigh.

"After Miss Bird batted her eyes at Gibbs, he swore he would work it. He has found *nothing* thus far," he grumbled. "Go bother him. I'm not working this case. In any case, women lie far better than men." With an air of finality, the detective yanked up a broadsheet to separate us into two factions. Sherlock quickly pulled it back with the top of her cane, revealing the peeved face of Lestrade once more. The space around us quieted down, anticipation filling the air. Sherlock leaned in.

"One crown says we solve it before Yuletide," she challenged. Lestrade raised an eyebrow, conscious of the eyes around him. He stood up and extended a hand.

"Deal's on." The two shook on it. "Gibbs! You've got two passengers on your sinking ship."

A few detectives that I recognised from some of our other joyful encounters with the Yard laughed with Lestrade who, himself, resumed his hard work by leafing through his paper.

74

Gibbs, a man with thin brown hair and a bushy brown moustache, popped out from a consulting room on the other side of the room. His eyes were caught in a wild look as he waved at us.

"Holmes! Watson! Come, come!" he waved us over manically. "I could use an extra pair of eyes and ears."

We were ushered into a room with a massive corkboard, eleven statements surrounding the edges. There was also a list of eleven churches. We inspected them all and found what Lestrade had concluded about the different depictions of the man – each physical appearance, tone, and accent of voice was different from the other.

"A mastermind, it seems," Sherlock said definitely impressed. "A prolific actor."

"It is highly unlikely to be just one man," Gibbs remarked, shaking his head. "I believe it is a troupe of men, all of which have colluded in order to steal the futures of several beautiful ladies." At this, he crossed his arms – expectant of our reaction no doubt.

Sherlock looked at me. I lifted my shoulders.

"It is a theory – better this than to be without one at all," I said.

"If they were a group then, it would be rather unusual indeed for no two of them to be similar in accent or physical appearance," she smirked. "Most friendship groups do share a commonality of class, career, marital status and, in some cases, even a shared hobby. Whereas these gentlemen all range from different walks of life – from the highborn noble to the dreaming artist."

Gibbs looked dejected, "So, you think it not a group then?"

Holmes shook her head. "I believe that to be very unlikely, Gibbs."
Gibbs pressed his lips together.

"Any other observations?" he said, his voice hopeful.

"The churches – are they all based around London?" Sherlock scanned the board. A flicker of a smile crossed her face and I knew she'd spotted something. She raised a finger and ran it across the map of London.

"That's right, Holmes," Gibbs said wiping his sweating brow with his sleeve. "Though I don't suppose he will strike again – eleven girls is more than enough bounty for one man. And no other girl has come in."

A thought struck me then. The girls were all from different regions of London – how had they come to know each other's misfortune?

I voiced this concern to Holmes whose eyebrows furrowed.

"The papers!" she burst out. "They put out advertisements looking for their prospective beaus. Hence why our Casanova was so keen to move from place to place –

to avoid any rumours of spectacle following him." Sherlock clicked her fingers and ran a circle around each of these areas again.

Gibbs nodded. "Yes, but we are still no closer to finding the smarmy bloke."

Sherlock paused.

"In order to find our gent, we need to find out how he knew the girls' situations," she said. "None of these ladies are highborn, their personal affairs would not be aired in anything scandalous. How did he learn of the demise of their fathers?"

"Perhaps he knew them all?" I suggested. "An after death carer? Perhaps a morgue worker or hospice staff?"

"Could be. But how would he know of the family's financial situation?" Gibbs asked, his face hopeful. Certainly, a morgue attendant would only know the bare bones of the situation, the cause of death, and the family to which the deceased belonged. It would take too much time studying before proceeding with his dastardly plan.

"And how would he know to woo the daughters in such a way that would be effective if he didn't know them before?" I added, upon reflection.

"He knew their sicknesses and situations. I believe he shared your profession, Watson." Sherlock cast me a glance.

"A doctor?" I exclaimed. The thought of such grave misuse of the Hippocratic oath made my stomach churn. I quietly promised the villain a piece of my mind when we figured him out.

Sherlock, who had barely sat down a moment since our arrival picked up her hat, cloak, and cane.

"Come along, Watson. And you, detective," she directed at Gibbs who leapt to his feet and gathered his belongings with the speed of a steam engine. "This was your case before it was brought to us. Together, I am certain, we can solve it."

We both knew it was she and I that would solve it, yet it was a nice gesture to Gibbs to include him in the investigation.

Miss Bird's house was in a lovely area of Chelsea indeed. We heard the chatter of many female voices. It seemed she had gathered the rest of the jilted ladies for us to interview upon Holmes' call ahead of our arrival.

"Mr Holmes, Mr Watson – and Detective Gibbs!" Eliza exclaimed as we appeared on her doorstep. The congregation of women behind her fell silent. "Come in, come in. We've been expecting you."

The presence of so many amiable young ladies took dear Gibbs by surprise and he blushed a shade of red reserved for beets.

"Right then, ladies," Holmes said clapping her hands together. "We need details of each of the doctors that served your families."

Just like that, one by one, each of the girls gave the same statement of an older gentleman with a nearly bald head, small squinting eyes, and thick eyeglasses. He also had a bushy moustache and spoke in a Scottish accent.

"Such physical appearance must've been a further guise. However, he has slipped up here, using the same one with each of the ladies. For someone as proficient in disguises as he appears to be, this is a severe misstep."

"He covered large areas of London in order to pull off his schemes," I said, shaking my shoulders. "Changing from one persona to another for each patient would require a fair amount of work."

Sherlock nodded. "Or perhaps he started with this guise and didn't change it after his first few successes."

One by one, girls dressed in pretty lace and cotton gowns walked to the table that Eliza had cleared for us to conduct their interviews. Each of them was pretty and had innocent faces but they all had the same expression of sadness in their eyes. I ached for them. All of them falling for the same menace. Though Sherlock had not spoken for a while now I knew from her steely expression, she was more invested in seeing justice done.

Gibbs finished completing the interviews of the ladies and had a list of different names for different doctors and places of residence. One particular lady had caught his eye. Miss Whitlow, a pretty girl with auburn curls by her shoulders had sent him a private smile that had him smiling from ear to ear. He realised we were watching him and he cleared his throat to compose himself. I bit my cheek to stop myself laughing as Miss Whitlow gave the officer, who was now a deep scarlet, a coquettish look.

"I'm not sure how helpful this is going to be, chaps," he said passing the list to Sherlock. She inspected it closely. She looked up at me, her eyes shining.

"Gibbs, there is an indistinguishable pattern here of residences all in specific places away around London," Holmes grinned and pulled out the map she had stolen from Gibb's evidence board. She began circling each of the residences with a pen borrowed from Miss Bird.

I saw the pattern right away. Gibbs, too, caught on eventually and rubbed his chin in shock. His eyes widened and he mumbled something about how he could have missed it.

"We can safely rule out any of the locations that he has his supposed office and focus on the place he had left safely away from his wrongdoings."

A circuit of streets had been completely omitted by our doctor – they appeared suspiciously boring. Sherlock's finger landed on them – Pimlico, Abbot's Manor, and the Gardens. Absent from all wrongdoings.

"This is where the rat resides," Holmes boasted.

"Time to smoke him out," I added.

The auburn-haired beauty offered the Scotland Yard officer some more cake. He had caught her eye – a Christmas miracle all on its own. We couldn't possibly pry him away as Miss Cherrie Whitlow had well and truly turned Gibbs' head. Sherlock informed him we would return to the Yard this evening with any news and telephone if we had any news prior to that, then left him to his merriment.

Holmes and I shared a knowing look as we left the terrace.

"Romance, Watson?" Holmes teased as we headed home. "You have a soft heart."

I rolled my eyes at her, but I noticed a tinge of pink on her own cheeks. In the
orange glow of the streetlights, she truly looked like a spectacle all on her own. The evening was drawing on and the frost was already beginning to crisp on the ground when we headed toward Pimlico.

"Shouldn't we retire for the evening, Holmes?" I asked as we progressed along the street. This whole area was residential houses that were newly built. Tall buildings with windows illuminated in a golden light as families enjoyed their pre-holiday suppers. Wreaths of holly and mistletoe hung under doorways.

A few other couples walked, hand and hand, around the pretty gardens. Holmes seemed to have retreated into her thoughts that it took her a while to answer my question.

81

"My dear Watson," she started, her eyes alight with the orange of the lanterns that lined the street. "I have a plan – but first we must lay a trap."

The following day, a room in Pimlico had been rented at no.7 Gloucester Street and an advertisement had been placed for a local doctor to aid the ailing father of one Abigail Rochester. Urgently.

Gibbs had called every doctor in this corner of London and told them to pass the message on to their colleagues. We had three doctors call already and Sherlock had given each a quick interview before sending them on their way with a pound each for the inconvenience which seemed to please them all. Gibbs, himself, had joined us from the station too. He spoke animatedly of his new acquaintance, Miss Whitlow. It warmed my heart to think some good may yet come from this dire situation.

"Holmes, if you are wrong and the gent does not show his face, I do not think the girls will blame you for it," he started to say, rubbing his hands together. The room was unfurnished, stripped bare for renovation. There was a stove that had been disconnected and there was no firewood about to light a fire.

"I am sure I am not wrong, Gibbs," Holmes gave one of her infamous crooked smiles, leaning against the doorway between the corridor and the drawing-room. "Give the gent time to ponder his newest lady."

Though pondering was advised, Gibbs remained unconvinced as the day drew on. We debated parting ways to lunch then reconvene, however, Holmes was determined not to leave until the gent had been caught. Gibbs disappeared to relieve himself around three o'clock, leaving the drafty house to ourselves.

"I did not imagine this is how I would be spending Christmas eve, Sherlock."
She hadn't spoken in a few minutes and I had taken the time to chew through a book I had brought to pass the time. Her eyes flickered open and sighed.

"At least we're with each other." Her voice was quiet in the hallway. There was a silent promise there, one that tied knots in my chest. Those silver eyes were as piercing as ever, but they had begun to look soft to me. Despite the arctic winds that echoed through this shell of a house, my heart was as warm as our open fire at 221B Baker Street.

I sent her a small smile, which she returned in earnest. We locked eyes with each other for several moments that seemed to last an eternity.

A stern knock at the door brought us back to reality. It couldn't be Gibbs. Readying ourselves, Sherlock and I assumed our positions. I cleared my throat before opening the door. There stood a balding man with a great bushy moustache. He wore pebble-thick glasses on his rather large protruding nose. He wore a black woollen coat and a thick dark scarf covered his neck. I nearly started as his appearance alone. His eyes were dark and narrow with wariness at Holmes and I. And I could imagine, if I was alone, he would've been an imposing presence.

"Good afternoon, sir," he started to say his voice was light with surprise. "I am sorry to disturb you. I am looking for the residence of Miss Abigail Rochester regarding an urgent call for care for an elderly man."

"Yes, sir!" I said, my lines scripted by Sherlock. "We are still conducting interviews for the right professional for the role. If you are interested, please step right this way." I pulled the door open wide and directed him to the sitting room. The man eagerly stepped through the door. Sherlock had already noticed the heavy similarity between the description provided by the ladies and he who stood in front of us now. She raised her eyebrows once to me as he made his way through.

He hauled a large doctor's bag made of leather so beaten that it must've seen plenty of use. I recognised the stamp from the medical school at Imperial College. Even if the man were a fraud, the bag, itself, was genuine.

"How strange," the gentleman remarked, stepping into the lounge. "Are you Miss Rochester's brother?" He extended a hand to Sherlock who took it freely.

"I am her servant, sir." We had a chair set up for the interview already – one of the few items left in this house. "Now, firstly, what is your name?"

"Doctor Dixon," he provided, pushing his spectacles up.

"Have you ever met a lady named Miss Eliza Bird?" Sherlock asked, as blunt as a knife. The gentleman immediately stiffened.

"No, I have not," he grit out. "An acquaintance of Miss Rochester?"

"Indeed," Holmes smiled politely. "How about Miss Ethel Maynard? Or Miss
Cherry Whitlow?" She tilted her head.

The doctor clutched his bag.

The signs of guilt were as obvious as daylight. Sherlock was getting cockier by the second. She crossed her arms and scanned the quivering man before her.

"No, and I don't see how this is relevant," he said. But the game was already over. I stepped in front of the door. Gibbs, having surprisingly good timing, knocked on the door at that exact moment.

"We've got him."

The Doctor was a failed medical student turned actor named Arthur Declan. After failing on the stage, too, he was near destitution. At the police station, the evidence team analysed the chemicals retrieved from his bag. They found nothing but poisons and strong painkillers like morphine.

In the end, Declan confessed to the murder of eleven men. Though those men suffered from their own chronic illnesses, their deaths were before their time. Doctor Death, as we referred to him from then on, enjoyed the rest of his life behind bars.

Gibbs married Miss Whitlow the following June. After receiving a few letters from Sherlock Holmes, various governors decreed that the ladies could keep their houses a little while longer without the need to marry.
It must be of note that a few of them had sought Holmes' hand since then.

The Tiger at The Bay

It is true that London, sprawled out in every direction like the great roots of a tree, has provided the background to many of our tales together. However, some of my favourite adventures at Holmes's side took place further afield – at the very heart of Britain. The great country of Wales has borne enough of its own tales, as old as the hills themselves and the castles that guard them. This tale is one of ours, yet there are no dragons here – only a tiger.

The air smelled of salt and sea. As the madness of the dock ensued in front of us, Sherlock Holmes took in a great big breath. She wore her favourite three-piece suit under a dusty black frock coat, on which she had layered a blue woollen scarf and a dog-eared leather cap to keep her ears warm. I had grievously misjudged the weather and rubbed my hands together in fear that if I stopped, for even a moment, my blue fingers would snap off like dead twigs.

Cardiff's docks were a snapshot of madness. Great cargo ships that carried coal to the world, streamed from the port. Vendors brought trade in, making the place smell of soot, burning oil, and fresh fish. Sherlock and I had departed the train moments before and my legs still shook from the constant jostling of the rails and from being rumbled in a carriage for a better part of the day.

We waited for the constable by the paddle steamer berth at the bay. Constant streams of Welsh conversations flitted between English words and undiscernible chatter. I could also hear French, Norwegian, Spanish, and Italian as we weaved our way through the crowds. It was the first Saturday of the New Year and already January felt frostier than ever. I vowed to purchase some gloves and a more adequate coat upon the conclusion of whatever business Holmes had dragged me away from the comfort of Baker Street's open fire for.

"Ah, the sea!" she declared, loud enough that a few patrons of the dock turned their heads our way. Of course, my companion paid them no notice. "My big blue friend! How are you?" She spoke with such conviction I wouldn't have been surprised if the sea responded.

"I don't believe the sea can vocalise a response," I said, crossing my arms over and pressing my hands into the warmth of my underarms. Sherlock gave me a flat smile.

"Nonsense," she said. "Look see – it *waved*!"

I glowered at her, biting back my smile. But before I could retort, Sherlock yelled in a voice so loud, I jumped.

"Rhys!" She waved her arms wildly as a gentleman came approaching us. He was a tall fellow with a top hat, squared shoulders, and brown frock coat. His white starched collar was high on his neck and he'd tied it with a red cravat.

"What a day! It's only bloody Sherlock Holmes!" he exclaimed, rushing over. She laughed and hugged the man back. He was built like a barrel and I had no doubt that under that coat was a wall of muscle.

"This is my partner, John Watson," Sherlock added after his great bear arms had freed her. I extended a hand which he engulfed with his glove. "This is Detective Rhys Lewis, an old friend."

"Good to meet you, sir," I said politely. He nodded at me and smiled kindly.

"And to you, my good fellow. Thank you for travelling all the way down to see us! How was the train?"

We exchanged pleasantries for a few moments longer before Holmes and her friend began to catch up. Reeling off tales from a time before our paths had crossed, I found the stories of a younger Sherlock to be much similar to those of her now. Her wily, chaotic thoughts and wilder actions made great tales when read aloud. Yet, I did notice a shine in Mr Lewis's smile – his eyes softening upon looking at Holmes and, though he was polite to me, he seemed more in tune with her. As they caught up I smiled to myself, wondering what sort of spell my companion had cast on this man.

Its potency had clearly not yet worn off.

The station was a little further inward from the dock. The short building was partly swallowed by the heavy foliage that grew over its right side; patches of damp had grown into lichen on the bricks making the whole thing look dank.

"Excuse the state of the place, sirs," Rhys said, his positive voice tightening. "It is hard enough to keep any semblance of order here and do the housekeeping as well."

"I can imagine," Holmes said and I agreed. Rhys opened the door wide for us.

The port's hustle and bustle must have kept them busy. Many corners of Cardiff Bay looked as if they had fallen into disarray. Paint had chipped away with time. Dead flowers hadn't been replaced from their beds, and grass was overgrowing in public plots. The fast-paced nature of the business conducted here clearly took priority over maintenance. We entered the main floor of the station. The noise hit us first – chatter, the drumming of so many footsteps, and even weeping emanated from behind cluttered desks that belonged to the officers and detectives who worked here.

Lewis lead us towards the back, to a small room the size of a matchbox. There was a desk and two metal chairs wedged in here, along with files of all sizes scattered over every other surface. We had to manoeuvre around each other to reach our seats.

"As you can see," Lewis gestured, "we are in dire need of a major update…." Then he mumbled something about finding the right file and instantly dove into the pile on his desk. He produced a thick, bound case and slapped it in front of us. Sherlock leaned over and picked it up. A picture was what greeted me first.

"As you can see, gentlemen. I did not bring you here to simply enjoy the beauty of Wales." He was quiet for the moment as I analysed what was in front of me. "We– I need your help."

The case was full of pictures of dead men. Their deaths were all equally gruesome – a blade across the throat that cut the jugular in half. The account of day, time, and kind of man all varied. No one shared the same walk of life or upbringing as the last. Sherlock and I read each of them as Lewis fed us more information.

"The locals have dubbed the murderer 'the Tiger'." He folded his arms on top of the desk. "The killing blow is always the same – the claw mark."

"Why not the 'Dragon'?" Holmes pondered aloud.

"Because they don't exist," I told her matter-of-factly. She shook her head at me, unabashed.

"Tigers don't look like they could exist either," she replied. "Big cats with striped coats seem like something only a child could conjure. However, just because they aren't around now doesn't mean they weren't around at some point."

Lewis shrugged at that.

"It's mainly because of what the locals have begun to call the town – Tiger Bay," he said. "Things are mad around here when it comes to criminal activity since there's constant buzz and trade. Hence why this part of Wales has garnered quite a reputation."

"Tiger Bay, hm?" Holmes mused. "A fierce name, indeed."

"How do you know that the Tiger has killed all of these men?" I asked leafing through each statement and picture. "What suggests it is only one man?" Surely, a group would be more adept at killing at such a scale.

Lewis rubbed his stubbled jaw.

"They all have something in common. The same way of death – it's a symbol of arrogance and a claiming of the dead. This is what I believe anyway." He sighed. "Yet we have received neither hair nor tail of the man."

"What is there to say it is a man?" I retorted back. "Both genders have been afflicted by this killer. Surely they would have no preference."

Lewis's eyes narrowed ever so slightly. He glanced at Sherlock as if looking for aid but found none.

"I have gathered enough intelligence on the sheer gruesome nature of these murders to suggest that it is a man. Being that *most* of the gentile sex could not handle such gore and blood." With that, Sherlock raised a brow and opened her mouth. Before she could snap, Lewis jumped in again, "Unless you both find something different."

Sherlock snapped her jaw shut.

"There is another reason why." Lewis pulled out a smaller file and flipped it open for us to see. "We collected these fingerprints off the last victim."
My eyes widened. I had read about the research following this! It was all still so new that I had no idea it was already in practice. Out of the corner of my vision, I noticed Sherlock's eyes lit up.

"Goodness! I had no idea that the Welsh police force were quite so up-to-date with foreign research," she exclaimed. Lewis gave us a bashful smile.

"Ah, you see there lies our problem," he clasped his hands together. "Our newest mortician has got quite the brain for these things. He is away on business in Taff's Well, but I shall introduce you upon his return. It isn't official evidence thus we cannot convict on it alone – we need more than just a match."

Holmes grinned as she regarded the DNA prints – a genetic marker system that was completely unique to one person.

I reached for another print, myself. The sheet was thin as tracing paper; I held it tentatively.

Sherlock's smile was wide as we both silently appreciated the research that had produced such an impressive collection of data. Considering how rudimentary the practice was at the moment, we relished in our shared awe.

"Have no fear, Rhys," she spoke. "Murder cases are second to none in London. Crime is a language we both understand too well. Isn't that correct, Watson?"

As usual, she gave me too much credit. I couldn't disappoint the conviction in her eyes.
"Elementary, Holmes."

We took rooms at The Royal Hotel in Cardiff's city centre and shared a twin room of plush double beds. Our window looked out onto St Mary's Street. We knew from our exploration earlier that right at the top lay Cardiff Castle – a great stone monument to a time passed. Its current owner was in the business of restoring it. We had peeked in through the gate and seen the tiny Viking castle in the centre – the yolk of the egg.

Sherlock had promised me a proper visit of the grounds when our business with this gory case finished. We laid out the files on the floor in chronological order alongside the witness testimonies.

"All men," Sherlock wondered. "Clearly they all upset the wrong person." She clicked her fingers, pulled a picture from the start and one more recent. "Hm. Same family."

"Mr Will Jones and Mr Dafydd Jones," I said, lining them up side by side. "That's unlucky."

Sherlock, who had pulled her pipe from her luggage and lit it, made a noise of disagreement.

"No coincidence," she tutted. "They all had something connecting them – the rest of the family may be able to give us a closer idea as to what it is. Then we can figure out the motive for their murder."

It took a moment to find the Jones's residence, being that there seemed to be many in Wales who shared the same surname. And first name... We found them eventually on the corner of a residential estate that the locals called Grangetown.

The houses here all looked the same. They were an unending chain of red-bricks that all seemed to lead back to the docks. There was little refinery here, one got more of a sense of unity amidst chaos. Houses wedged in between themselves as to best preserve space. These terraces seemed to go on forever.

We found the house quickly. There were some plants kept in pots by the door that appeared well-kept. Peonies and poppies made a pretty arrangement despite the grey of the sky.

Sherlock rapped on the door twice. A short, stout woman with dark hair opened the door. She sported puffy cheeks and purple half-circles under her eyes. I removed my hat in respect and Sherlock was quick to follow. I had nagged her upon social etiquette before, yet she only seemed to recall the unspoken rules when it best suited her.

"Miss Jones?" I asked. "Are you the mother of Dafydd and Will Jones?" I kept my tone as gentle as I could muster.

"Yes, they were my boys," she said, giving me a grim smile. "Are you from the station? Detective Lewis mentioned he'd send someone." Her eyes darted between the two of us.
"Yes, my companion, Doctor Watson, and I are on the case," Holmes said with a polite smile. "May we come in?"

She instantly stepped to the side, beckoning us in.

"Of course, of course, sirs. Sorry, I didn't expect you for quite some time." She lead us into a small sitting room

95

with a fire burning in the pit under the chimney. There rested a copper kettle and a hotplate. "Can I get you some tea?"

The living room was a state. Sheets were thrown over armchairs, clothes resting on air dryers above the fireplace. If I looked for them, I was sure I would find rats here, too. There was one thing no city could avoid – poverty.

"No, thank you, ma'am," I politely declined.
Holmes shook her head too. Her eyes were inspecting the place; her brows low as she focused on every detail. I knew she was looking for clues, but someone could just as easily misjudge her eyes as scornful.

We perched on the edge of a battered set of furniture. I got my notebook out for notes.
"When was the last time you saw your sons?" Holmes asked, pressing her lips together.
"Will was first – last August," she started, her brown gaze focusing on the carpet. "Then Dafydd disappeared in November. He didn't come home from work on the 5th. I had a feeling, then, that the Tiger had got 'im."

We learned that the boys worked in the same trade, helping out a business in Swansea called Taff's Coal to sell their wares. They would negotiate sales of sacks for ships to take them out to Europe. Miss Jones's eyes shone with pride as she recalled. The docks were the last place they were both seen.

Neither of them had wed. The elder, Will, was only twenty-one years old, his brother – nineteen. Holmes narrowed her eyes at this.

"Who were their elders in the company?" she pressed. "There is always a common ground in killings like this. It is just a matter of figuring out what it was."

Miss Jones said nothing, simply bit her lip. All of a sudden there was a bang at the door as a young boy and girl walked in. Their faces were dirty and their clothes too.

"Ma! Ma! Tabby climbed up the hill by the docks and we almost walked all the way to Penarth!" The young boy reeled off their explorations as, I assumed, Tabby took him by the ear and into the kitchen, speaking in hushed voices about the bobbies. This display of normality seemed to have eased Miss Jones' features. Her shoulders slackened and the corner of her lips twitched into a tired smile.

"Tabitha and Garyn," she explained. "My youngest two."

"Do they know what happened to their brothers?" Holmes asked. Once I would've winced at her bluntness, yet I've grown accustomed to it since our companionship began.

"They know they are not returning," she said in a quiet voice. "A work accident is the official story. I would appreciate it if you refer to it as such."

We both nodded.

"May I have the name of his employer? Any friends?" Holmes inquired now that the subject was apparent. "They may know more as to any more private hobbies or…

indulgences that they may not perhaps share with their mothers."

Miss Jones winced and stood up abruptly. She dithered a moment before scuttling out the room. There was the noise of an opening drawer, things being shuffled about. Just as I wondered if we had offended her, the woman returned quickly to where we were.

"I meant to bring this to Mr Lewis but since you pair are here, maybe it is better in your hands." She carried a small wooden box with two rudimentary bronze snaps on the front. It had a carver's mark which I didn't recognise so I quickly assumed it was locally sourced. "It belonged to Dafydd – I found it under a loose floorboard under his bed."

Sherlock pried the box ajar ever so slightly before slamming it shut. I didn't get to see the insides. Before I could open my mouth to protest, she shot me a look that silenced me on the spot.

"I am sure you know, sir," Miss Jones was addressing Sherlock, her expression grave, indeed, "if that box is what I think it is…" She didn't finish her point as Sherlock spoke instead. My companion's face was just as stricken.

"Indeed, ma'am. I think this concludes my questions." She nodded once at the lady in front of us before snapping her attention to me. Was it something that grotesque to invite such shame?

We quickly exchanged pleasantries before Sherlock herded me out of there. I barely had time to close my notebook

98

and tuck it back into my pocket. She strutted on at such a speed, I had to double my pace to keep up.

"Heavens, Sherlock! What is it?" I pressed, catching up just in time to catch her by the arm. "Are you well?"

My use of her first name pulled her from whatever thoughts had taken her. She blinked twice and rubbed her forehead. My palm slid off.

"Don't be so concerned," she berated me, but I could tell there was no heart in her words. She clutched the case in front of her. "This case may, indeed, be more difficult than I had previously estimated."

"What's inside?" I asked. Her face instantly pulled back, her entire body rigid. Sherlock took several steps away from me.

"Holmes!"

"Not here," she hissed. "Back at the hotel."

"Is it that revolutionary?" I hissed back, the cold air was burning my throat. Her expression was tight but her eyes shone.

"This changes everything, Watson."

I could barely get anything else out of her on the rest of the journey back to the hotel. Finally, our feet found St Mary's street. As soon as we were through the door, I crashed onto my bed and kicked off my shoes.

Sherlock's aquiline features looked a ghostly grey. She sat on the floor, the box at her feet. She waved me over, her hand swinging wildly. Her piercing grey eyes were only focused on the box. A curl of anxiety travelled through me.

Finally peering inside, we found a roll of parchment-like paper and crushed powder pressed into balls or rolls. I knew instantly what it was. Sherlock had snuck these into our apartment more times than I could count.

"Opium?" I breathed, my words barely audible but I felt Sherlock nodding. "In Wales? I had no idea it reached outside of London." The phenomenon had clearly breached the borders here – laudanum, all of its bonuses and negatives, had grown their roots here, too.

"Clearly," Sherlock muttered, her gaze still on the contents of the box, "someone is capitalising on this trade. The killings are related, undoubtedly. I assume the victims were all dealers. Look closer." She beckoned me with a hand, pointing at one of the pressed balls of powder – there was a signet pressed into the white. I distinguished several large petals and a black centre.

"A poppy," I replied.

"A Welsh poppy," Sherlock added. "This must be the signature of whoever the maker is." She moved the contents of the box around gingerly, checking to see if there was anything we had missed. Under the rolling paper was a box of matches, something scrawled on the front.

"Adelaide Place, November 5th – 11 o'clock. The Swinging Mermaid," I read. A horrible stone feeling sunk in my chest. This was where the younger Jones had met his fate. "A base of operations?"

"Only one way to find out," she said with promise.

Cardiff Bay looked beautiful at night. Indigo waves lapped against the shore. Boats bobbed in their docks as drunken sailors took up space on the pavements, tankards in hand, their voices filling up the cold evening air.

"Can you imagine living here?" Holmes mused, her eyes tracing the long line of coast. It teetered off into obscurity if you followed it far enough along the bay. "There is something to be said about the beauty here."

I looked at her strangely. "Only you could say that while investigating a serial killer."

She tsked me. "Why should I let one person spoil something wonderful?"

There was something to be cherished here. The sapphire blue waters and the beat of life that seemed to be sung on a sea-shanty made my heart feel light. Part of me wished we were just here to enjoy the scenery – just the pair of us. Sherlock had an uncanny ability to look completely at peace wherever she was. Wherever we went, you could guarantee one thing: she would wear it well.

We sped along to Adelaide Place. The place wasn't well kept and the smell of both beer and urine stank enough for Holmes to pull a face of disgust. I pulled out a handkerchief to breathe into.

The Swinging Mermaid was a small shack of a pub hiding at the end of the terrace. Its windows seemed slanted and its door was nearly beaten off its hinges. There were sailors fighting in the road. Young, scruffy men, and ladies in cheap silks with torn tights jeered them on.

Holmes didn't pay them any heed as she entered the establishment, leaving me once again to chase her. My upbringing had left me a snob, yet I was wise enough beyond that to note when a place was of ill repute.

A band was playing some popular jig that I recognised on fiddles. Couples copulated in the corners whilst the drunker patrons swayed in their seats or dribbled on the tables. We took up a place at the bar, ourselves. I was hopeful that the sheer volume of bodies would disguise us. However, I still the hair on the back of my neck stand up and encountered more than enough eyes on us upon looking about the room.

"Hello gents," the barkeep greeted us. He appeared a man in his forties with brown hair streaked with grey and a round red face. "What can get you?"

Holmes raised her eyebrows in surprise to find him standing there. "A scotch and a whiskey on the rocks, if you would."

The barkeep nodded and got started on our drinks.

"I don't think we will find anyone here – it's too busy," I said, sidling next to her. She narrowed her eyes at me and the corner of her lip twitched. "Do you even have a plan?"

"Really, Watson," she teased, "I never have *one* plan."

Before I could reply, the barkeep came back with our drinks. I brought out my wallet and paid for them.

"Good sir, do you know where I can find Dafydd Jones?" Sherlock asked. The barkeep stopped counting the shillings and focused on Holmes instead. She spoke in a tone that could only be described as cheerfully oblivious. "I have come from London to buy goods from him. A friend of mine worked the docks for a while and came back with something I found most intriguing."

The bartender did a quick sweep with his eyes before beckoning us closer. I tried to ignore the grotesque stickiness of the countertop as we leaned in.

"The boys in the corner over there," he said, pointing to a group of men in waistcoats and flat caps. "They'll sort you out."

As if by magic, but was most probably what I assumed a secret signal between the men, we were approached by a young man with yellowing teeth and pupils that were too wide. He stood to one side of us while another of his men, chewing a fat tobacco cigar, came up behind me. My heart sped up. I took my whiskey and drank it whole.
Holmes's smile was wonderfully ignorant as the man spoke.

"Hello there, Detective Holmes," he said. I noticed more black teeth in the back of his mouth. "My boss would like a word with you. In private." He glanced at me, his grin sending a shiver that raked my body whole. I sent daggers to Sherlock who seemed delighted by this revelation.

We were taken through to the back of the pub. There, they bound our hands together and tied our feet to the chairs. Across the room was a woman in a silk dress with purple embroidery and a bustle. Her face was heart-shaped, adorned with full red lips and rouged cheeks. Even her shoes reeked of wealth that could rival Saville Row.

"You were foolish for coming here, Holmes." She glanced at me then. "Doctor Watson, I presume. I do love reading your tales whenever one of my scouts brings me back a copy from the Strand. It is a shame, really."

"You can't kill us," I said, deadpan. Everyone in the room let out a chuckle – including Sherlock.

"But if I don't, I wouldn't be able to carry on with my good work here," she said.

"Let me be so bold to assume you to be Mrs Lemmings," Holmes said with a smile that bared her teeth. The woman's eyes widened. "I recall reading about your husband in the Telegraph, ma'am. And that you went missing during proceedings."

She barked out a humourless laugh. "How clever you are, Holmes."

"I am, aren't I?" she grinned. "I knew from the moment I saw that pack. I knew that someone from London had infiltrated Wales, and through the Bay no doubt. A few murders of your drunk mules here and the Tiger was born. The symbol alone was enough to scare the locals into carrying out your misdeeds, wasn't it? Alas, then they became the Tiger."

"Kill him," Lemmings barked to the one closest to us. The boy looked no older than seventeen. He had a switchblade in his hand. His face bore a strange look of unease.

"Have any of you seen this Tiger?" Holmes asked matter o'factly. The younger boy froze in his place. I assumed Mrs Lemmings had brought the two men flocking her from London as they appeared older. The divide between them was there in age, which allowed the distrust to set in.

Around the room the young men started exchanging looks with each other, their twitchy faces looking between Holmes and Mrs Lemmings. The one closest to the door suddenly flung it open and bolted out. Mrs Lemmings let out a yell and slapped the boy next to her. Commanded him to finish us off. He edged towards me. I hadn't got out of my ropes yet. My breath caught in my throat.

What happened next happened so quickly I could not even see it. Sherlock shrugged off the bonds off her hands and jammed the knife upward by pushing the boy's hands up high. His fingers faltered on the knife, letting Holmes twist it free. She elbowed the boy in the guts and stood in front of me – the knife in her hand.

The boys who had realised their folly ran out of the room only to be intercepted by the familiar voice of Detectives Lewis and half a dozen men. I assumed this was the note she had left at the reception for him. The group was quickly apprehended, along with the stash of opium that they'd hidden in barrels under the bar.

Holmes untied me and brushed me off before I thwacked her in the arm.

"Next time, you tell me the plan," I reprimanded her. She simply shrugged her shoulders.

"I didn't know how it was going to go down," she said. My stomach lurched.
"We could've died!"

"Nonsense. I had at least twelve back-up plans that would've stopped that." She looked at the rope. "I told you that skill would come in handy."

I scowled at her. I had not forgotten the times Mrs Hudson had walked in unexpectedly after Holmes had made me tie her up. It was part of her new practice: escapism. Naturally, she was brilliant at it whereas I was terrible. Yet she insisted upon me trying too. Trying to explain why Holmes had left me tied to a chair in three in the afternoon left me with rope burns, a red-face, and a laughing Mrs Hudson.

Lewis saw Mrs Lemmings and her crew behind bars. The fingerprints belonged to one of the gentlemen in her inner circle – a man named Bryn Howard. After questioning, we learnt that each man belonging to the Welsh Poppy gang had been blackmailed into service, else the Tiger would've killed their family. With enough murders under her belt, none of these men stood against her.

Meanwhile, Holmes made good on her promise as she and I went to the castle together.

We returned to Wales many times in our cases together, but Tiger Bay never lost its name.

The Burning Hen House

February was a month full of love for many – in the forms of family, a job, a pet, between husbands and wives. And the scandalous loves too – love of vice; love of money; and the kind of love you pay for.

A scandalous individual who knew of the pleasure houses of the Spotted Horse may have also traversed through the Theatre Royal in Covent Garden and enjoyed an experienced lady, full of red-hot desire, for a reasonable price. I knew Sherlock, herself, may have traversed such a place before she'd met me.

My occupation as a doctor meant that I was called wherever needed. I had no mortals to betwixt or wife to scald me. I only had Holmes, who offered to accompany me whenever my skills were required. One such instance was when a fire had sprung from the pleasure house, King's Station on Knightrider Street. I asked if she had been there before, but only received a tsk in return.

"Not for that," she declared. "For a case, a while back. A lady there was embroiled in a scandal involving the Tsar of Russia, a stolen relic, and an iron." She didn't elaborate as she grabbed her top hat on the way out. I grabbed my own cap and pulled my coat over my shoulders. There was a haste in her step.

The area was a well-known one to me. I had serviced ladies for other problems that may afflict them and once I made it clear I was a friend, not foe, the women of the midnight hour passed my name around. This position garnered admiration from my other friends in London, who appreciated the charity but also earned me the disdain of snobbier nobles of the view that these women were damned creatures.

We turned the corner from Godliman Street and there Knightrider lay in front of us. I nearly gasped at the sight. There was charred furniture in front of the house, a chaise lounge lay toasted black and some sad cushions were half-ash on the cobbles. Silken sheets lay on the ground, having been suffered the same fiery fate. The smell of melted fabric and scorched wood was unpleasant, mixing with the perfume that lingered about every item.

Holmes's eyes were wide.

"A small fire, you say?" she commented. I followed her line of sight only to gasp at the burnt-out window from which fire had stretched a shadow of soot upon the red bricks. "Perhaps they had been modest about the scale of the fire."

Two beefy gentlemen, one with heavily tanned skin, the other pale with a mop of dark hair, dumped another lounge chair in the street. All that was left of it was a skeleton.

"Perhaps, it started as only a small fire." My stomach was tying itself in knots. I rushed forward to the doorway with Holmes on my tail. The next thing the men brought out had me nearly topple over at the sight of it.

Both men hauled out a wooden trunk. The outsides of the box were unscathed by the fire, but steam was coming out from inside. My insides dropped as I took hold of the human figure that lay there, terribly burned – enough so that his face was raw red, his mouth lolled open, the jaw blasted wide. The figure emitted no noise. I knew it was too late. I clenched my hands by my side and steeled myself. Sherlock squeezed my shoulder as a means to comfort me. Before I could turn to thank her for the small gesture, out stumbled a familiar face, flanked by two officers in uniform.

"Lestrade!" I shouted, pulling the detective's attention to us. He came over at once, eyes wide, his usual arrogant candour replaced by obvious discomfort.

"Detective?" Holmes addressed him, raising an eyebrow. No doubt she'd already drawn her own conclusions. "I thought you only dabbled at Madame Fitton's in Bridewell Place?"

Lestrade's face instantly fell, back into its usual disdain for us and, for once, I felt relieved to see it. He gritted his teeth and send a glare to the officers at his sides that was enough to threaten silence.

"There is no time for such quack from you, Holmes," his beady eyes set. "Doctor, I see you've got your bag with you – I think your services would be much valued in the drawing-room."

I didn't wait to correct him. I only nodded and made haste to the second room to the front of the house. A collection of grey-faced girls were sprawled over the stairs. Each girl was covered in soot and ash, their faces sharing looks of horror and fatigue. I took my hat off in respect.

"Doctor Watson?" a young redhead at the top called out. Dirtied faces all turned in my direction. With a clatter, she stepped over her sisters at work, landing in front of me. Besides the smattering of ash across her features and her torn, dirty nature of her dress, I recognised her instantly.

"Lottie, is that you?"

Her bright blue eyes lit up and she nodded her head quickly, pulling me in a tight embrace. I felt myself freeze for a mere moment. Recovering, I patted her on the back, and she pried herself away. Lottie Gelbum had come to me for a rash only a few weeks prior. Then she'd been employed in a smaller brothel across town. It was only a mild allergy to lavender that had caused the rash, cured easily with a few creams. I found a kindred spirit in her kind eyes and bubbly personality.

"Oh, doctor!" she cried, wiping her eyes and then her hands on her dress. "Quickly, come see Alberta."

She ran off towards the back of the house. I dodged various ladies and gentlemen on the way, who looked at me in surprise. Laid out on a mattress in the kitchen were two girls, both groaning. Their bodies were horribly burned, hands a raw red. One had suffered terrible wounds across her thighs and legs.

"Oi! What do you think you are doing here, sir?" A boisterous lady in a cotton red dress with a grim expression whirled on me. Before I could retort, she continued scolding me, "No business today! There has been an accident – sling yer hook!"

I ignored her, kneeling by the first girl with the more severe burns.

"Ma'am, this is Dr Watson," Lottie explained. "We called for him earlier. He's not a customer."

The lady, who I assumed was the Madame of the house, flung her arms into the air before crossing them and staring me down from where she stood close to the door. Now, I could focus properly on the patient I evaluated her state carefully. I moved the hair on her cheeks away from her burns gently. The girl, whose hair was dark, and complexion pretty, hissed before forcing a laugh.

"I could definitely do worse than this one. Surprisingly, pretty features for a gentleman," she giggled and then coughed.

"Lottie, please get me some cool water and clean towels." I took off my coat, folding it over a nearby chair. I rolled up my sleeves. The other girls had hushed to hear me work. I cleaned the wounds before emolliating them with some healing ointment for burns. Then I bandaged the girls thoroughly. The first one with dark hair was Alberta. The second, with the lighter hair and freckled skin, was Helen. Helen was in better shape in comparison to Alberta who had a deep wound on her head – perhaps some timber had fallen on her?
"How did this happen?" I asked as I finished bandaging the hands of Helen. Alberta had been propped up with some cushions to help her breathe. "Were you there when the fire broke out?"

"You sound like an officer, Dr Watson," Helen said as I gently wrapped her fingers.

"It was an accident."

"Hmm. Indeed."

There was something amiss here, I could see it in the girls. Even Lottie was holding something back, clenched between her teeth and tongue. It must've been a matter of importance. I wondered if it were because of a specific person.

The Madame did not appreciate my presence in her kitchen regardless of the fact I had already been sent there. Under her watchful eye, none of the girls dared divulge any more facts on how the fire had started and how it had spread.

"Don't forget about the corpse," Holmes came up from behind me. She had a shine in her silver eyes, and I knew that she had a lead, a plan, or something she was excited by. "Nice to see you working in an environment comfortable to you and your skill set."

I checked over the bandages on poor Alberta's legs. "Isn't the kitchen floor more of your environment?"

"How rude." But a smile graced her lips. She was now actively on her feet, scanning the kitchen. Holmes approached the sour-faced lady of the manor. "Madame Gerund, I presume? I am Sherlock Holmes, a consulting detective. My friends at Scotland Yard are looking into the murder that took place here."

One of the girls on the stairs gasped. A murmur went up among them. Either they didn't know, or they were surprised someone talked.

The Madame stuck her nose in the air.

"And I will tell you what I told them," she snapped, "it was an accident. There was no *murder* committed here." She stumbled over the word as if it shook her as she said it. Holmes was unmoved and tilted her head a little to the side. The lady was outraged but clenched her fists. "I will discuss this with you further in the parlour, Mr Holmes." She glared at Lottie who hopped up from where she was kneeled next to me and immediately went to lead Sherlock out.

"This way, sir," she said politely. Sherlock gave her a polite smile but shook her head.

"I'll wait for my companion. Watson always takes the best notes."

Madame Gerund's face flushed and her voice hitched as she spoke.

"Fine. I will meet you there. Show them up when the doctor has finished his work, Lottie."

I gave Sherlock a glare that questioned the necessity of riling up the woman when she may or may not have been an accomplice to murder. My companion only wriggled her shoulders a little and winked. I ignored her.

I finished checking Alberta's bandages and informed her that I would be back to change them. The girls had to take care when bathing in order to avoid getting the bandages wet thus preventing infection.

I looked to the other girls. Sisterhood was common in places like these and judging by the expressions on the other maids' faces, I was sure that Alberta and Helen would be well cared for.

Lottie ushered me upstairs. The girls had somewhat migrated in order to follow us, while some of them had gone back to their own rooms. One could easily see and smell where the fire had started from the scorched wood near the front of the house. The door had been propped open and the room cleared, its former contents laid out in front of the house.

Two rooms had been devoured by the blaze. The damages in the second, made the first's wounds look minuscule. There was nothing left that had not been roasted beyond repair. The bed, itself, was a thing to behold – a skeleton made out of mahogany held the remains of what used to be a mattress. On the floor was a collection of grit and dirt that made my body tense.

"It is quite a sight to behold, is it not?" Sherlock said over my shoulder. "The girls are lucky the rest of the house didn't collapse. Thankfully the sheer volume of individuals here were quick to put it out. Alberta alluded to some of the clientele helping, fearful that their favourite task may be put at risk."

"There is no way this was an accident." The ferocity of the flames, the unexplained death, the way everyone stood on edge… Something bigger was at play here.

Holmes hummed in agreement.

"For once, Scotland Yard is in line with us." I raised my eyebrows at that. "My thoughts exactly."

She narrowed her eyes at the four-poster bed. "But if the Madam is arrested and hung, the girls will be destitute. Turned out onto the street."

I thought of the girls, of Lottie and her unending joy. A pit clenched in my stomach and I clung to my resolve. I glanced to where she waited by the parlour, anxiously hopping from one foot to the next.

"We must first understand it. Regardless of how grisly it may be."

Madame Gerund waited with a stony expression in a room with whitewashed walls and tall beige drapes that were patterned with flowers. There was no bed, only a collection of lounges, chaises, and chairs. A jumble of blankets lay close to the open fire. It, in turn, was filled with logs to fend off the bitter spring air.

I sat down next to Sherlock who was opposite the bawd. The lady's lips were pressed together thinly.

"Why don't you start from the beginning? I could retell it, but I need refreshing on all the details," Holmes said. The woman looked as if she would rather burn herself, but she took a deep breath in and smoothed out her skirts around her.

"Firstly, *Doctor*," she said in a tight voice. "Here at King's Station, we allow all kinds of company for any paying customer. Naturally, our girls are from all over London, and beyond. Each of them is very good at providing whatever a client requires." She paused to clear her throat. "The unfortunate soul was a regular client called Roderick Edgar. He always came to visit Miss Alberta – whom you have seen is downstairs in a sorry state." She huffed a sigh, a vein in her forehead popping. Her hands clawed into her dress. "Her career has no doubt been shot to pieces by this horrible, disfiguring accident."

Her pain was evident, but I could not distinguish if it was pain over the injury of one of her workers or the perceived loss of value.

"What does Miss Alberta specialise in?" Holmes asked, crossing her legs. The Madam narrowed her eyes. "As in what do clients like Mr Edgar request when inviting their company."

"Alberta is a master of bondage. Patrons love the feeling of being out of control and a domineering figure being in charge. It's a popular fantasy," Madame Gerund said like it was a fact. Perhaps the day had done its course and now weariness was all she felt.

Living with Sherlock Holmes had given me steel for any kind of awkward scenario, yet I found myself reddening at such frank talk. Holmes had no tact when it came to anything others might find insensitive. If we were here as our female selves, no doubt we would've been shunned for vulgarity. Yet, as men, such talk was acceptable. I could not

117

shake, however, the learned behaviour of my finishing school days as easily as Holmes could.

"And on the day of his untimely demise," I spoke, the Madame's hard gaze on me now, "did he participate in such activities?"

The Madam's gaze softened for a moment. Perhaps she could see the awkwardness I was trying hard to conceal.

"Yes, Doctor Watson," she said. "I saw the man to Alberta's room – the destroyed one, not the informal drawing room which has already been cleared out." She sighed, shaking her head. "I left Alberta with Helen, as sometimes another girl must be there to… assist. Not even an hour later, they both began screaming. The door had been locked as the girls appreciate their privacy. They had lost the key, so they were just banging the door down."

The Madame rubbed her temples.

"Apparently, what happened was that Alberta had lit candles before the session. She'd tied up Mr Edgar on the bed, her back turned when the fire had started. Helen was tied up as well. Seeing the severity of the fire, Alberta looked for the key to go out and seek help. By the time we found the other key, Mr Edgar was dead. The fire was an inferno, the girls were both horribly burned."

There was nothing but silence in the parlour for a few moments.

"I hope that clears this horrible accident up for you, sirs. Now if you don't mind, I have my girls to tend to." With that, the lady excused herself and left Holmes and I alone in the parlour.

I shot my companion a look at which she burst out in laughter.

"Did you have to boil her like that?" I asked. "A man has *died*."

Holmes cleared her throat.

"When you were downstairs acting like God's servant on earth, the lady approached me with a number of her girls asking if I would like company." Her laughter became light. "Don't look at me like that. I did no such thing – I am happy enough with the present company I have."

My concern for the Madame waned. Clearly, she was more concerned about making a profit than the poor state her girls were in. I clenched my jaw.

"Let's go look at her room. Maybe we can see whether or not this was indeed an accident."

Holmes nodded and leapt up from her seat. She opened the door and lead us toward the remains of Alberta's boudoir.
"If it were not for the dire burns the girls had suffered, I think it would be a safe assumption to theorise that they were part of the murder."

"I think we can safely rule their participation out. No woman of the night would damage their way of income for a murder."

The crisp door shut behind us. The burns inside were horrific.

Being in the room itself gave my imagination life. I could picture Alberta and Helen having their way with a man. But how did the fire claim them and the room so quickly? The pools of wax dripped near the beside confirmed my suspicions and the Madame's words.

"Candle wax."

Holmes nodded. But the session had been an early morning one so why was there a need for more light.

"Candles at dawn, however?" I cast a look to the fireplace. The walls nearest to it were heavily burnt – this was surely how the fire had spread.

"I don't believe the girls would've needed extra light, if that is what you are thinking Watson. I believe it was something to do with more of the activities they were using them for."

I pondered for a moment. Surely the candles would not have been used for more than adding to the sensual atmosphere of the mood. Rose scented candles were popular among ladies as were lavender ones, as they released pleasant aromas.

"Perhaps it was a request from the customer," I said. "Madame Gerund did say they were very accommodating."

Holmes crossed her arms, leaning forward to the crispy headboard.

"I have an idea what the candles were used for," Holmes said. She crossed her arms. "You might blush again, dear Watson." She added, because of course she noticed from earlier.

"Enlighten me." She gave me an even smile.

"I will ask your friend Lottie later if I am correct – I believe the wax is dripped upon a person. To... Liven the senses."

I kept as placid a face as I could. I could not decide if it sounded horrifically like torture or deliciously sensual. Holmes measured my response – lest she try it on me later.

"So, if we entertain this idea for a moment. If Alberta did this practice frequently, surely she would know to be careful with it." I looked to the droplets on the floor. "Why didn't she have a bucket of water or a safe way of preventing any accidents?"

Holmes did not get a chance to reply as there was a quick rapt at the door. Lottie rushed in and slammed it shut.

"Lottie?"

She placed a finger across her lips to silence me.

"I am sorry, Doctor. The walls here are ever so thin and I thought I could be of help while Alberta and Helen are resting." She looked to Holmes and nodded. "Wax is not something new to clients like Mr Edgar. We buy soft candles for the practice specifically, so the wax will not burn them – only give them a pleasant little shock."

Lottie crossed her arms in front of her. Her ears pinkened and she avoided my gaze.

"I have accompanied Alberta before and I must say the practice is very popular with more... unusual clients, whose tastes are a little outside of the normal company."
Holmes's eyes lit up.

"Without making poor Watson combust with vulgarity," she teased, gleefully ignoring my glare, "please run us through a standard session with a client such as our poor Mr Edgar."

My stomach clenched. Nothing fazed Sherlock because I knew she had done it all before. She had men when she dressed like a woman and she had women dressed like a man. I didn't need verbal confirmation – she knew everything anyway; but on this subject she knew too much. It made my stomach drop to my knees. For I knew the biology of it all and everything else was speculation.

Lottie spared me a sorrowful glace before she began.

"So, first there is the usual drinks and kisses just to get them feeling amorous and eager. Maybe slightly tipsy too." I could imagine that was a common tactic to loosen the control the gentlemen had on their wallets. I crossed my arms across my chest.

"And then?" Holmes pressed. "You lead them up here and engage in the risqué proclivities that your colleague Alberta specialises. You tie them to the bed in some form and engage in all the fun activities that the customer has signed up for. You tire them out, have them pay and then send them off to church?"

"How did you know?"

Holmes waved towards the remaining iron frame of the bed.

"There are indents where force has been applied. One could assume the ropes would not be strong enough, but something solid like iron chains might do the job." Her voice was filled with something beyond her deductions.

I peeked at the top of the frame and saw some crescent-like dents in the scorched metal.
"If playing with fire was part of the routine for Mr Edgar, why was there no a precaution, like water, nearby in case things went awry? To put a customer at risk is something that could ruin Madame Gerard's entire business." I thought of the ropes. "Unless it was part of the request."

"But it wasn't, was it?" Holmes got in before Lottie could say anything. Her blue eyes were round like a doe's. "There is a very faint line in a circle of where, say a tin bucket would be placed in case anything went south."

Of course, she had noticed something like that. As I peered down, I saw it too.

"So, as the fire was not put out, why was the bucket not put there for this client?"

Lottie gasped, a hand flying to her throat. My heart sank at the noise she made. Her gaze zipped from Holmes to me, eyes watering. Her chest heaved, raked by powerful sobs.

"I swear I filled it up! I had everything prepared and I double-checked it was under there."
"You're sure? Holmes will be able to tell if you're lying."
As if on cue, Sherlock hummed behind me. Lottie's face was frozen in sadness and fear, but a flash of hurt crossed her features which made me clench my jaw. I hoped Lottie knew this was just part of the other role I played for Holmes.

"I'm certain, sirs," she said in earnest. "Someone always checks it is full.

Holmes pursed her lips.

"Then it is like I thought. Alberta has a wound on her head, yes? And Helen was, from what I perceive, judging by the marks on her wrists and the fact she didn't see anything, that she was blindfolded and tied up too?"

Lottie hiccupped as she cried. "Sometimes it helped a client relax if they were doing it with them. He would've been blindfolded too."

124

Holmes went to the window which was open just a little. She slid it up. It was remarkably untouched by flame.

"The window frame is damp," she said. Snapping her fingers, she stuck her head out and reached down, pulling up a gold pendant in the shape of a shamrock. "How many cats roaming the roofs of London wear 24 karats?"

She looked at Lottie, then at me.

My response was instantaneous.

"It was murder."

We left the house after I had checked over the patients once more. Night had crept in. Had we been at home, we would have been sat having dinner at this moment. However, Lottie's tears had left an uncomfortable feeling of responsibility to see the women's names at the brothel cleared. I was sat with her for a time before our departure while Holmes had riled up the Madam beyond repair with questions. One this was certain - whatever had occurred during that morning, I was certain Lottie wasn't involved.

We decided to visit Lestrade at the Yard to see if his research had brought anything new to light.

"The window was damp so surely this was to avoid it catching fire too, yes?" I said as we neared the heart of London. "Alberta must've been wounded by a projectile that succeeded in knocking her out and starting the fire. Why does the Madame claim it's an accident so viperously then?"

Holmes looked at me with regard – like I had impressed her for once in my life. She shook her shoulders as we reached the dark wooden double doors.

"Clearly she thinks one of her ladies is the culprit. Gerund doesn't want to sully her business' name with rumours that the girls kill paying customers."

The station was writhing with criminals, officers, and detectives as per usual. We had to weave our way through to find Lestrade sat at his desk, taking notes over a file. I recognised the yellow print of a mortician's report.

"Ah, finally I see you two again," Lestrade said with a smile that reminded me of the baser natures of men. "Did the women in Knightrider see you too off happily?"

I couldn't hold back my scoff as I dropped my doctor's bag on his desk with a clunk.

"Lestrade, some of us can handle ourselves around beautiful women and not become a mewling kitten desperate for milk."

His face fell as around him people hushed.

"They are murderers in that house, Watson. That Madam killed him for his coin and set the fire while the girls were in there. I suggest you do what you usually do and hold your tongue," he said snippily. "But I suppose you and Holmes here think otherwise, just to be contrary."

Sherlock, who had a look of surprise on her face, suddenly remembered herself and narrowed her eyes at Lestrade.

"On the contrary, we know otherwise, Lestrade. The bawd would not damage a prized earner like Alberta or Helen. The bucket of water stored under the bed for accidents had been poured out the window prior to Mr Edgar's arrival. Someone knew he was going to be there and, after disposing of the water, hid under the bed to await the right moment, strike Alberta – hence her head injury, then douse Edgar in oil and striking a match."

She pursed her lips. "That is what your coroner's report says, is it not?"

Lestrade sighed and defeatedly shut the case file. "Right, time to find the suspects."

We left it to Lestrade to find out where Mr Edgar lived, and we reconvened there the following day.

I found myself in a foul mood as we arrived at a pretty street in Blackheath. The houses were all well-kept and dressed in flowers. Yet my attitude would not subside despite the pleasant scenery. I gritted my teeth as we reached Mr Edgar's residence.

A lady dressed in mourning clothes with a veil over her pale, withered face.

"Good morning," she greeted, her sallow face sunken with grief beneath the dark drape of net. Her age had curled her hands and thinned her hair.

Lestrade introduced us and she immediately led us into a dimly lit parlour. The inside of the house was a different story compared to the outside. The furniture was shabby and worn, but still, the woman looked as if she lived comfortably.

"I couldn't believe it when I heard," she said raising a silken handkerchief to her face. She looked to Holmes and I. "I am sorry I cannot offer refreshment. I gave my servant the morning off the grieve. She should be back soon."

"Never mind about that, ma'am," Sherlock declined politely, waving a hand. "Did you and your husband have a healthy relationship?"

"It was happy, mostly." Her voice was quiet. "I know he took his pleasures elsewhere, but he was never cruel to me. He always did the best he could."

I didn't say anything. It was not my place to, as it was her life. However, I didn't agree with whatever Edgar must've put her through.

"And do you have an alibi for yesterday morning?" Lestrade pressed on. Mrs Edgar nodded.

"I was staying with my cousin on Fleet Street, Miss Margaret Smith. Truthfully, I am glad he is gone."

Lestrade's eyebrows shot up.

"He didn't seem happy here with me anymore," she elaborated, wiping her eyes. "He was always quick to leave for work and was almost never home. When he did return, it was never for long. There was a gap in age between us – it never mattered at first, but eventually, it was what separated us."

There was a moment of silence among us before Holmes spoke again.

"It seems to me that perhaps you are now free of the worries he gave you." It wasn't accusatory just stated. Mrs Edgar looked relieved at the statement and my heart softened a little.

Sherlock reached into her coat pocket and brought out the shamrock necklace which she had wrapped in an old cravat for safety. "Tell me, ma'am. Do you recognise this?"

Miss Edgar brought it up to her face and let out a gasp of recognition.

"I thought I'd lost this years ago! It was a gift from Mr Edgar from when we were courting – he said it would always bring me luck when he wasn't around."

I shared a look with Sherlock. Lestrade's face grew pale, but thankfully he had the tact to stay silent.

"Your servant, ma'am," I said. Her eyes rested on me now. "How long has she been in your service?"

The lady let out a laugh.

"Oh, forever," she admitted. "We kept Miss Rees from the second year of our marriage. She's a good girl, six and twenty years of age." She smiled and looked truly at ease for a moment. "Still as radiant as ever, though."

We waited until Miss Rees returned to question her. The girl had been Mr Edgar's mistress for years. As she confirmed our theory of the events at the brothel, her face took on a complexion as hard as steel.

"He lied to me for months. I would do it again and burn all those creatures with him. Have them ride him to hell."

I had to excuse myself while Sherlock and Lestrade informed Mrs Edgar about what had occurred. Once outside, I could hear her sobbing from the street. I couldn't tell whose betrayal she was upset with more – her husband's? Her friends?

Lestrade called officers to escort Miss Rees from the property and had her processed in Scotland Yard. Our carriage ride home was one steeped in silence. Holmes had a pressed look on her face as we came into our familiar home. She wouldn't meet my eyes, instead she stared out at the gloomy sky.

The steps up to our quarters made my heart thump with every step. Holmes went in first and shed her coat before hanging it on the hook.

"Tea?" She asked looking to the kitchen.

I hung up my coat too. My stomach felt like a bed of worms. I couldn't open my mouth to talk to her. Everything felt tense. This space between us was too close.

I stepped into my room and slammed the door behind me, shedding all the trappings of my male alter ego and unbound my chest. Replacing my shirt with a cotton vest.

There was a knock at my door. I didn't reply.

"What is bothering you?" she called from the hallway. Her voice was surprisingly forceful. I didn't reply as I rubbed the skin that was now free from its coverings. "I'm coming in then."

She pushed the door open with gusto so much that it banged on the wall.

"If you are mad at me then speak now." Her expression changed when she saw my face.

"I have no patience for this today," I said through gritted teeth.

She didn't move. But she did join me in taking off her male facial features.

"I can deduce many things, however, women frequently allude me."

"What is this, Sherlock?" I said, standing up now. I gestured between us. Her eyebrows shot up. "Am I just Mrs Edgar, minding the house until the right thing comes along? Are you just going to leave when you do?"

She was taken aback. Her voice lifted.

"What are you talking about? I'm not leaving," A horrible feeling curled in my gut and I felt sick with envy, with worry. I hated every second of it. "Are you jealous?"

For a second I worried she might laugh at me. I couldn't take my eyes off her, even as mine welled up. We'd slipped into something together – I couldn't even pinpoint when it had happened. But I'd had this feeling in my chest something light and warm that fluttered whenever I looked at her. It was beautifully agonising.

"I don't even know what I am to you," I said. Her expression had become pained, tight.

I turned to the window. I needed air.

Before I could take a large gulp of fresh breeze, Sherlock grabbed my arm and pulled it so hard that I crashed into her. Her other hand caressed my face, briefly, tenderly, before our lips met.

The kiss was soft and made my knees weak. She pulled away from me all too soon. Our brows pressed together and we locked eyes.

"Everything," she breathed. "Don't ever question it. You are everything to me."

Once Upon A Murder

The afternoon sun warmed the lounge as Sherlock and I ceased our fencing. Lowering our sabres, I exhaled a warm breath and pulled my helmet off with my free hand. I proceeded to collapse into my armchair. Holmes laughed at me as she took off her own helmet.

Outside the snow had fallen deep and white, but I couldn't feel it beyond the heat I had already worked up from our exercise. I wiped the sweat on my forehead off with the back of my gloved hand.

"It is pleasing to see your head is not always in the clouds, Watson," she smiled, taking her protector off. I rolled my eyes. "You make far better competition first thing in the morning. Less yawning, more parrying."

"You work me raw, Sherlock. Sleep crucial for my brain function."

Sherlock never needed to rest as I did. Sleep seemed optional for her. Even if the case were lengthy, she would stay up until the sun rose, and only then would she consider rest.

Sherlock's cheeks were pink, her breathing fast. Neither of us had dressed in male garb this morning so her short hair fell about her face. She grinned, showing me all her white teeth before collapsing into her own chair, hooking both of her legs over one of the arms. She had bought a set of swords from an antique dealer on Portobello road and decided that we should both become proficient in swordplay. Conveniently, she was already a master at fencing so it was not too much of a difference apart from the sword's weight.

"Being right is crucial for mine," came her response. She took the jug laid out on the table, poured a glass, and handed it to me.

"Thank you," I said before gulping from it. "Any thoughts on the case?"

Sherlock sighed through her teeth.

"As satisfying as it is besting you in battle," she started as she poured a glass for herself, "I have had no revelations about the murder." Tapping her fingers against the glass, her brow furrowed.

"Blast. I thought we would have solved it by now."

Our flat was messier than I liked to keep it but sometimes Holmes liked to spread out her work over every available surface. That included the floor, the table, the kitchen and the bathroom – before I had her clear it. Becoming completely immersed in the facts helped her think. Or so she claimed.

London's winter season was incomplete without its share of snow, scandals, and shows. Thus, as we were called to the theatre, we were met with a gruesome sight. A particularly gory affair of the demise of one R.J Abrams.

He was one of the stars of a harlequinade – a rowdy play telling of The Grimm Brother's *Little Red Riding Hood*. He played the role of the wolf after he pretends to be Little Red's grandmother – a scandalous, lewd version that made the crowd roar. The act would run as follows: the wolf, upon reveal of his disguise, would pounce on Little Red. But, unfortunate for him, she's stolen a broadsword from the woodchopper. Clearly, the writer had taken some thematic liberties when it came to the original tale. Then Little Red would "stab" the wolf in the neck several times and the Grandma would pop out from the wings and all would be well in Fable-Land once more.

However, this time as Little Red discovered her grandma was not just unseasonably hairy and was, in fact, a blood-thirsty wolf, she brought the broadsword down and swiped the man's head off his shoulders in one fail swoop. The crowd had thought it part of the play and were in stitches with laughter as Little Red skipped on stage. The girl, seeing the blood, had fallen unconscious on the spot. It was only when the crowd ceased laughing did the screaming begin. The theatre was cleared, leaving Mr Abrams, a grandmotherly-dressed stump, on the floor in a puddle of red.

Little Red was played by a substitute that evening as the original actress lay sick with scarlet fever. The new girl had only just met the individual tonight. The sword, it turned out, had been very sharp, indeed. It had dropped to the stage with a clatter before later being lost in the flurry of feet running out in fear.

It seemed the poor Yard was just as stumped as to the victim. The night before last, Detective Gibbs dropped the case at the door, along with the promise that we spend our Sunday investigating it. Of course, Holmes was delighted. I, too, was intrigued with the case – gory as it may be. Despite our sex was usually confined to needlework and childrearing, yet solving murders was far more interesting to me.

After we had both bathed and drunk coffee, we donned our male disguises and headed to Scotland Yard. As per the December season, it was full of drunkards, harlots, and the smell of whiskey. Sherlock's nose wrinkled and she tried not to laugh as a uniformed bobby wrestled a drunk man whose trousers were bunched by his ankles. I shot her a look of disapproval. Yet, as the drunk vomited all over the officer and his desk, I struggled not to laugh myself.

"I love London," Holmes said, quickly weaving us through the mob toward the Commissioner's office. As we shut the door behind us the racket of riotous yuletide drowned out. The Commissioner was an older gentleman whose salt and pepper hair was swept over a thin patch on top of his head. A smile out of him was rare and gave an event significance.

"Apart from a traumatised cast and an audience of witnesses," Commissioner Clarke adjusted his half-moon specs on his nose, "there isn't a murder weapon to be found, and the only thing left at the crime scene was the body." His shoulders slumped. "Gentlemen, you have your work cut out for you."

"Do not fear, Commissioner," I said. "We are on the case and I am sure we shall find the perpetrator."

He nodded, yet the frown lines on his head seemed to deepen.

Sherlock raised an eyebrow and looked at me before leaning on her cane. "Sir, have faith. There is no need to feel downtrodden." The Commissioner pulled off his specs and rubbed his eyes and temples.

"Is there something else bothering you, Sir?" I asked.

Commissioner Clarke leaned forward, sighing. "My wife, Mrs Clarke was very much looking forward to seeing this cursed harlequinade. She has been jovial for weeks. It was to be an anniversary present to celebrate thirty years. Now she's going to have me swing from the gallows." He swallowed, accepting his fate.

Sherlock pursed her lips. I shook my shoulders. I had heard rumours around the Yard about the Commissioner's wife. Apparently, she was a formidable woman – one I had never had the honour of meeting.

"Perhaps a different show?" I suggested. "London is never short of showmanship."

The Commissioner shook his head. "She had her heart set on this one. No. I am resigned to my fate."

The corner of my lip twitched as Sherlock and I shared a look. We knew of a place.

"Have you ever heard of the Old Vic Theatre? It's a new endeavour in Waterloo."

"Yes, I heard. Opened by a woman, yes?" he said, moustache wrinkling.

Sherlock straightened. "Miss Emma Cons, if the rumour is correct. She had has monopolised the Royal Victoria Coffee and Music Hall. I have heard great things about the Shakespeare performed there," she continued to say.

Holmes and I had been there ourselves and enjoyed many a performance – on more than one occasion I had to nearly drag Holmes off the stage herself. Macbeth appealed to her curious desire to investigate superstitions.

"I still think I am destined for the noose, gentlemen," Commissioner Clarke paused, then waved a hand. "Though I will look into this theatre you have recommended."

"Perhaps, a dinner as well? As it is a big celebration," I added. "Thirty years should be marked by something special."

The man looked weary at the prospect of making more of an effort. "Be glad you are not married, gentlemen," he said. "You are very lucky."

"On the contrary, sir," Sherlock said. "A woman decided to spend her entire life with you. It is you who is lucky." She tipped her hat and spun back to the door. Her hand stayed on the door for me.

I bowed quickly as the stricken Commissioner recovered himself.

"Gooday, Sir. Congratulations again," I said, turning quickly on her coattails as Sherlock left the room with a flourish, as she liked to do. She waited until we were back in the brisk December air to speak again, rapping her cane on the pavement, her silver eyes alight.

"Bloody women."

We took to the Adelphi Theatre on the Strand. It was woefully empty. Bags of nuts and half-drank tankards of ale lay about the place. There were a couple of other officers investigating the scene. The headless body was dressed in a pink and white striped nightdress with a frilly collar and puffy sleeves, Abram's feet stuffed into heeled shoes with great ribbon bows on them. He was also wearing thigh-high stockings with lacy red garters.

The men near the body were sniggering. We traversed over to investigate them. One of the gentlemen had hiked the dress up the body's legs. I heard Holmes try to stifle a giggle next to me and I elbowed her. The red garters had clearly been part of a set.

"He was clearly very dedicated to the role," she said, clearing her throat. "Though I could've lived without seeing that."

I swallowed down a chuckle as we went to the head. It had rolled offstage after the attack and since then someone had propped it upright on a stool. The wig must have been pinned on quite well as it remained switched to the bonce. Tatty white curls clustered around a powdered face, tied with a head wrap. The faux dame's skin was plastered in lead white chalk, with his cheeks and lips stained in red dye.

As a doctor, I had seen enough gore to satisfy enough dozy lifetimes but this particular head made even my stomach clench. The neck was crusted around in blood with tendrils hanging from it. Eyes shut, mouth closed. The skin was leeched of all colour and the smell of decay already drifted through the air.

Sherlock looked closely. "The skin being torn this way definitely suggests someone's sword was professionally sharpened, requiring very force." Sherlock had an iron stomach and wasn't affected at all by the blood. She could happily ingest a full course meal around corpses. One time when we were in the morgue doing tests on blood after death, I caught her drinking red wine with cheese and crackers.
A gentleman in a red waistcoat greeted us. He told us his name was Antony Soot, the stage manager. His hair was shaved close to the skull, but he had long whispery brown hairs on his cheeks, chin and under his nose. His skin was red, his eyes bloodshot and dark smudges underneath.

"The murder took place at half-past eight during last night's performance," Sherlock thought aloud. "And no one has come in here since except everyone here currently?"

"Yes, Mr Holmes, Sir." Antony's voice was gruff. "The morning hours were watched by me where the body was undisturbed."

"By yourself?" I asked. Soot nodded, his jaw clenching.

"The footmen are afraid, and I couldn't get them to stay with me. My boy came and stayed with me. In case the shadow came back."

"The murderer, sir?"

"There is a rumour that this place is haunted. During one staging of Macbeth a few years ago someone else died due to a prop change. Only that time it was a pistol. Mr Gareth Healey. Such a shame…"

Sherlock narrowed her eyes. Ghosts were for bedtime stories. I had been given a lecture once when we were walking around Colchester Castle – she'd laughed in the face of our guide who claimed it was haunted. I spent the entire experience full of goosebumps, jumping out of my skin at the slightest creak. Sherlock made a mockery of me, frequently bringing it up to this day.

"Mr Soot, it is highly unlikely a broad-sword wielding ghost lives in your theatre," she said incredulously. "If anything, it was an accident by one of your cast."

The stage manager shook his head, crossing his arms. His nose twitched over his bristly moustache.

"Gentlemen, I was backstage when it happened," he started. He rubbed his forehead with his free hand. "No-one touched that sword last night before the performance. I didn't think ghosts were on God's earth until last night." He shuddered at the thought., casting a look toward the body. "Now I fear to be alone in here."

I didn't need to look at Sherlock to know her thoughts on the matter. I, on the other hand, couldn't help being swept along in paranoia. The shelves in Baker Street were full of stories of ghouls, goblins, devils, and beasts in all manner, shape, and form. Though I knew Sherlock took joy in poking holes in the tales, the thought of a ghost made the hair stand up on my arms.

Sherlock looked bemused at my expression.

"I think we shall assume the undead as a last resort," she said. "Where do you keep your props?"

Behind the thick red curtains opened the cluttered area where the magic of performance was made. Under the stage was a hatch door that swung open. Inside lay all the fake swords, guns, and crates full of stuff perfect for any performance. It was dark under there, yet no ghosts roamed about. Ropes and pulleys controlled the curtains and set designs across the stage. A vast collection of props lay neglected on the threadbare wooden floorboards that shone with the wear of feet. The smell of wood, polish, and sweat seemed engrained despite us being the only ones there. We could see the backdrops, some of which had been damaged in the chaos of the night before. Next to them were a set of mirrors of various sizes. Soot led us to the staff changing rooms alongside the storage spaces. One could really tell the age of the theatre from back here. There were scratches on the wall and floor, and the wooden brackets holding up the ceiling looked to be from the back of an old great ship.

A curious addition was the wall of signatures from stars and people dreaming of stardom who had scratched their names into stone. Curiously, a few had been blacked out with lead paint – I wondered whose reputation had been sullied enough to warrant such treatment. As Mr Soot found the keys to our victim's dressing quarters, I spotted a brazen signature in red ink on the brick and recognised the scrawl of Mr Abrams himself, Holmes tapped it with her cane. She lingered on the lead paint that was alienating his proud hand.

"Are the actors blotted out when they have caused scandal?" I asked pointing to the stripes of black marring the wonderfully reminiscent quality of the wall. Holmes lowered her cane, her eyes darting from the close proximity of the remembrance wall to the changing room.

"Or perhaps they offended someone in the theatre?" Holmes inquired, glancing my way.

Mr Soot scoffed.

"Not to speak ill of the dead," he said jangling the keys, "but Mr Abrams was a complicated character. He had many foes in his pursuit of the spotlight."

As if to accentuate his point, the stage manager opened the dressing room's door. Inside was total disarray. There were makeup pallets everywhere. Thick punnets of white face paints lay surrounded by dusty powder on the mirror table. Red lip pigments and a wig stand had been shoved on the floor. Shoes, clothes, and ribbons were strewn over every surface. Yet Soot didn't look at all surprised.

"Good heavens," Sherlock marvelled at the mess. "What war happened in here?"

"Another scuffle with two members of the public on the matter of some gin. The first man was down the pan,

144

smelling like a tavern. There was a black man there too – had him up against the wall. They fought and then the first man was dragged out of the premises. The other man ran off though. Something Gardner, I believe. He was taken to the station, completely tanked."

"Who was the other man?" I asked. This provided a motive – perhaps this other fellow was involved?

"Another actor who had a grievance with him," Soot said with a sigh. He scratched the back of his head, face becoming unreadable. "Abrams had a lot of problems working with other people and was very pretentious when it came to performance."

We inspected the room. Despite the complete mess, it told a clear story about the man who had inhabited. I found more bottles of gins tucked away inside his dressing room cabinet and a line of other dresses clearly made to his size. Sherlock found a few boxes of snuff with opium and tobacco in them, tucked away at the back of a drawer full of wig caps.
"Expensive tastes," she said, eyeing the white power pressed into cubes at the bottom of a mints tin. "What did his family think of his escapades?"

"He took all his pay upfront at week's end," Mr Soot shrugged. "What he had, he whittled away on bottles and bawds. I know I've had to kick out more than one set of harlots from here. As for a family, I don't believe anyone could put up with him off the stage enough for marriage."

"What about his parents? Siblings?" I asked. Relatives were still a better conclusion to a vengeful ghost.

Holmes had a glazed look in her eye as she took the place in. I recognised it from home – it was how so processed data and made deductions.

"Like I said, Sir," Soot sighed. "I didn't like to associate with the man. He was full of spite."

The body was wrapped up and taken to a morgue at St. Thomas's hospital. We thanked the superstitious stage manager and left him mopping the puddle of blood up with a tin bucket. He crossed himself before he started – a fraying look of fear and weariness rubbed away at him. All that was left of Abrams now was a pair of buckled shoes in size eleven and a foul reputation.

It did not take us long to track the man named Gardner. He was the newest resident of the drunk tank at the Charring Cross police station. We were shown to his cell by an officer who left us with the keys if we wanted to perform interrogation. Sherlock swung the keys like she really was debating going in there until the officer disappeared and she tucked them into her pocket. I had no doubt that it would be a different story had I not been present.

The man in front of us groaned as he noticed us. He threw a hand over his face, rubbing his eyes. A disgruntled expression stuck on his face. The night had taken the joy of drink and left him with only the searing reminder of the raucous events before incarceration. He was fair-haired, with an oval face with pale skin and blue eyes. He would've been attractive if not for the ugly scar marring his cheek; it looked like it had been branded on his skin. He was wearing riding boots and a torn red velvet jacket. There were dark circles under both of his eyes and his lips were staunchly pale.

146

"Mr Gardner, yes?" I asked him, leaning towards the bars.

"The one and only," he said begrudgingly – wincing at the noise.

"Detective Sherlock Holmes and Doctor Watson, sir," Sherlock greeted, perched on her cane. "We are investigating the murder of one R.J Abrams and hoped you might be able to help us."

Suddenly Gardner let of a hearty belch. He slung his feet off the bed and stumbled forward to where we stood. The smell made me long for fresh air. He rubbed his head and winced at the light.

"He's dead?" He poised a finger at us. I nodded. At this, Gardner slowly started to sway and then to dance. He said some very expletive words not meant for any polite company, then proceeded to do a sort of jig around his cell. I heard Holmes chuckle and perhaps I was trying to stifle one myself. Shock can do many things to a person but usually dancing is not high on the list of actions. I wished I had my notebook to sketch – Sherlock's face was a picture I never wish to forget.

"How did he die? Fall off stage and break his neck? Did one of his many lovers decide now would be *a prime* time to shoot him dead?" He then clasped his hands together and praised the Lord.

"Mr Gardner, you must admit this looks very suspicious," Sherlock said, her eyes alit with amusement and her lips twitched at the corner. "One does not usually dance at the announcement of another's death – especially when they've been murdered."

Gardner leaned through the bar and let his arms drape through the gaps he spoke in a refined voice that mimicked Sherlock's.

"One does indeed when that person was a money-grabbing, soulless whore with no heart or decency." He swung backward.

"So, you are saying it was not you?" I asked. His blue eyes fell on me. "After all, you have given us ample proof that you had great distaste for the man. And you were seen at the crime scene by multiple witnesses. What about the other gentleman with you? The black man."

"I was in the company of drunks; he was one of them. After my brawl with that fishmonger, you may ask the tavern owner at Hogshead for my alibi," he said with a grin.

"You could've paid someone," Sherlock countered. "People have done more surprising things for revenge."

"Yes, I could've – if I had any money," he scoffed. He gestured to his tatty clothes. "What you see is what you get. No one wants to hire a cursed actor now, do they?"

Sherlock leaned back on her cane. I looked at the mark on his cheek. Gardner's shoulders drooped as he turned from us and crashed back on the edge of his bed.

"Bad luck is not a curse, sir. I'm sure you will find a job soon."

He scoffed at my words.

"That cockroach of a man did this to me," he pointed at his cheek, rubbing at the scar. "He told everyone I was blighted and tried to cut the affliction from my face. That was a year ago. His career flourished whilst mine dwindled, then died."

My heart sank. Gardner was gripping the mattress so tightly, his knuckles had turned white.

"Nothing can be good all the time or life would be dull and predictable. You've just got to have faith things will get better."

He looked to me and before dropping his gaze to the floor.

Sherlock's brow furrowed.

"We know he was unpleasant, and I am sorry you've been through an ordeal. But can you think of anyone else who might have the means and intent to murder him?" She pressed.

The actor leaned back onto the bed. "The list is as long as my arm. But you might want to start with his wife first – I can't think of someone who would want to kill him more."

"Ah! So, he does have family," Sherlock turned to me, raising her eyebrows.

"An unfortunate family, indeed," Gardner said. "Last I heard, the wife had moved to a shack in Devil's Acre. I'm sure you'll find her there."

We had him write out the names of the other suspects and we thanked him when it was done.

"You know, if you don't find them – I'll be your scapegoat," he said grimly. He shielded the light from his eyes. "A hanging would be a blessing right now."

At this, Sherlock rolled her eyes.

"No one is doomed unless they decide to be," she said, tipped her hat, and went to leave. Instead of immediately following, I stepped closer to Gardner.

"When you are released from here, head to the theatre at Waterloo," I said. "The Old Vic. Speak to Miss Emma and tell her that Watson sent you. She will be able to help you."

Gardner shrugged his shoulders and judged my expression before replying. "Well, it sure can't get any worse."

Tipped my hat at him. "Good luck and goodbye."

"Goodbye gentlemen," he called before collapsing back on his bed.

As I left the cells, I swear I saw the ghost of a smile grace his lips. Maybe it was the foreshadowing of one.

That afternoon we took a quick lunch at Marcie's café on Buckingham Street. The public record offices had very little information on Mr Abrams. His residences in the back end of Belgravia proved fruitless upon our investigation. The landlord was a reedy gentleman with a groomed moustache that left his residences to their tenants' own whims. He had no knowledge that the gent was a player, and certainly wasn't aware of any family. According to him, Mr Abrams had rented the room upon the pretence that he was a bachelor; he certainly acted like it according to the other residents. Having found no record of him even having a wife, we headed into the waste that was the acre.

Devil's Acre lay by the houses at Westminster; it was a bog of a home and the smell was putrid with rotting food and human waste. How anyone could live here at all was beyond me, but I was too learned of the world to know that not everyone was dealt the same privileges as I.

"This place is huge," I asked as we reached a spider connecting various shanty homes together. "How do you propose to find them?"
Holmes walked like we were in a glorious park in the sunshine, rather than a place smelling of dung and faeces.

"The old-fashioned way."

Our taxi had let us walk in, the driver refusing to go through. The houses here were made of every material imaginable – propped up with bricks, sticks, mud, moss. They seemed to slant on their own accord. Individuals perched in the common spaces of benches made of old pallets, barrels, and the like. Those inside huddled around fires of their own making. One could hear any tongue muttered here, could collide with every nationality – London was a hive for business and dreams, and people from all over flocked here.

We got off in a side street with a name too smudged in grime to read. As we moved, whispers followed us alongside sideway stares. The police force had never been welcomed here – I could guess at the vices held in the shadows. I could see them, smell them burning and hear them hollering as we passed.

"Gentlemen! Fancy a pair of lovely ladies for your pleasures?" Two approached us, their bosoms buxom and pushed up in the discomfort of their corsets.

"Not today, ladies," I apologised, tipping my hat in respect. "Do you know of any Mrs Ambrams?"

The ladies of the night shook their heads.

"You can call me anything you want, pretty boy," the shorter one said. She had a tuff wispy hair styled upwards. I wasn't expecting that response. I tipped my hat again and scuttled after Holmes, who was busy laughing to herself.

"Come on, pretty boy," she said as we turned a corner. "I should lend you my Keats – it'll have them swooning over you. Not that *you* have any issue doing that when you blunder like that."

"Do hush yourself."

We found a group gathered by a lit bonfire in the centre of the shambles and asked if they knew of Abrams' wife. Our search was fruitless; for an hour no one could even answer us. Eventually, we found a man perched on the pavement with an apple in one hand and a knife in the other. He was cutting small slices away at it, cherishing every piece. He pointed us to a hutch on the corner of the street close to the Thames.

The roof was falling in and mould had crept up the external walls. My stomach lurched at the smell of damp and rot. Even Sherlock drew out her handkerchief and put it to her lips.

"Hello? Is anyone here?" she called as she knocked on the dark wooden door. I heard some shuffling inside but there came no response. "Mrs Abrams?"

A drawn woman opened the door. Her collarbones were sticking out of the ragged dress she wore. You could've hung onto the steep cuts of her cheekbones.

"That is not my name, I am Louise McLaren. But yes, I was that louse's wife," she rasped. The woman coughed and stumbled backward. Suddenly another figure caught her; a black gentleman quickly helped steady her upright. He was dressed in greys and, by looking at the white dust on his fingers, I could tell he was a steelworker.

"Good evening, Miss," I said. "We are sorry to disturb you. We are investigating the murder of your husband."
The woman's pale blue eyes turned watery. The gentlemen's face fell relief and astonishment was clear on his face as he placed a hand on her shoulder.

"He's dead?" her lips trembled. Sherlock nodded.

"Good God," the man muttered behind her. She turned and the two embraced. She wiped her eyes and gestured for us to come inside.

The shack was comprised of three rooms. A big living space with an area for cooking, with a copper tub for washing in the corner. The other rooms appeared to be bedroom spaces. The floors were piled with furry rags and knitted blankets. Pots and pans were littered about the place. Clothing hung above the fireplace to dry. A mantle had been shoved in the corner. I noticed the smell of the hot copper that was heating water on the fire.

There was nowhere to sit; a horde of children resided everywhere. There must have been at least six of them. The biggest seemed to be around ten while the smallest was a child with brown skin in a cradle who was fussing in the corner. Louise shoed the children into the next room so we could talk. She sat next to the baby and the black gentleman took her hand, kissing the back of it.

"Forgive the state of our home," she muttered, sad eyes looking about the place. "We never have guests."

Sherlock shook her head. "It is perfectly fine, Miss." She stiffly perched on the edge of a wooden chair by the fire. I joined her on a stool. "We caught you unawares."

"What was your relationship with the deceased, Miss?" I asked. She placed a hand on her head.

"We were in love when I was young – he was quite my senior, so I believed him to be wise." She frowned, her delicate face turning harsh. She scoffed. "I was stupid and naïve." Her face turned soft and her eyes dim. "My mother and father worked at the theatre where he performed, so I was there all the time. He taught me Shakespeare and I fell for him."

She freed her hand from the gentleman's grasp next to her. He looked at her with an unreadable expression on his face – his jaw was clenched, eyes on the floor. My heart dropped to my stomach. Sherlock had a focused look on her face. I tried to keep my face impassive, but I felt so bitterly sorry that I am sure it showed.

"I knew he had a tempestuous nature, but I thought he was different with me. I thought I would be able to change him." She sighed, shaking her head; like she was waking up from a bad dream. "After we wed, life with him became unbearable. He drank all of our money and beat me when he was upset over not getting jobs."

I felt rage for her. Even Sherlock's calm exterior slipped as I saw her gloved hand grip the cane a little tighter. The woman took a deep breath before continuing.

"I became pregnant quickly and he was repulsed with me. Called me nothing better than a sow and forbid me to leave the house. I ran away from him," she confessed. "I had to. I couldn't bear it anymore."

A new figure entered the room – it was a tall elderly woman. She sat down gently, a pipe in her hand, in a moth-bitten chair which squeaked under her weight.

"This is my grandmother's house, Maggie McLaren."

"Maggie! You should not have gone out again! Remember what the doctor said–" Louise's male companion started. The old woman hushed him.

"I'm already dying, Simeon." She breathed in a long draw of tobacco. "What is the worst that can happen?"

Sherlock continued to question the pair of them as the older woman smoked like a chimney in the corner of the room. I looked at her lean hands – tall figure, yet slight form.

"When did he die?" Louise asked. Looking at her frail state, it seemed one breath later and she could've passed from this life to the next. But the fire in her eyes made me believe that. The man gave her hand a squeeze.

"Last night, Miss," I said. "We were hoping you could help in identifying the killer."
"Where were all the members of your household last night, Miss?" Sherlock asked.
"I got in at work in the small hours, Sir," Simeon said. Louise gave a wry smile.
"I was up in the small hours too as having this many children is a job all on its own."
I cast a look to her mother who caught my eye. She winked at me. "I was in the tavern until midnight, then I came home and went to bed – a good Saturday night if you ask me."
Louise rolled her eyes. "Getting tanked doesn't help your condition, Mother."

"On the contrary, every wise decision in the history of England has been made whilst somewhat boozed."

The corner of my lip twitched.

"What was your relationship with the victim, Miss?" I asked Louise. Sherlock glanced my way, tilting her head. I could see the cogs turning.

"I was a stagehand long before that louse infected that theatre," she said, scowling. "He was a cruel man and he threatened to kill Louise after finding out she was moving on with Simeon." Sherlock and I shared a look.

"He did?" I asked the pair of them. Simeon's fists clenched. "He told Louise that she was an embarrassment living with someone like me."

"He was a terrible human. Hades roast him for all I care." Maggie said before taking a long draw from her pipe. The smell of freshly burned tobacco filled the room.

"Maggie, please," Simeon exclaimed. "They are still with the police." Maggie grinned with her pipe between her yellowing teeth, "What are they going to do? Arrest an old frail lady? Kill me? I alright have that in hand, dearests."

I liked this lady a great deal. I cast Sherlock an amused look and the twinkle in her eye affirmed that she agreed with me.
"Do you all have alibis for last night?" she asked, everyone nodding in unison.

"I went to work and came home late," Simeon said, firmly.

Sherlock cocked her head to the side. "Can someone corroborate that?"
Simeon stiffened. "I was the last person there. I am staying later to save up for our own place."

My companion and I exchanged a look. That didn't mean he had an alibi. He had enough reason to want to kill him. Motive and no alibi.
"Simeon wouldn't have killed him," Louise said incredulously. "He hasn't even ever been to the theatre."

"Actually, there was a brawl with the deceased before he was murdered. The first perpetrator was a man called Gardner, an actor."

"And a black man who got away," I said slowly.

Louise's mouth fell open. "That could be any black man! London is full of them." She shook her head. "Right, Simeon?"
Simeon took a moment, completely frozen. His dark eyes connected with mine and I knew the answer.

"He *threatened* you, Lou," he said. "He was going to hurt you."

Louise began to tear up and hunched over her knees. "You complete fool," she said, her voice thick with emotion.

Sherlock said nothing but her eyes fell on the elderly lady smoking a cloud in the corner. In front of us the pair started to row. Louise's face staunched and her eyes started to water again.

"I didn't kill him! I just wanted to scare him and get a good hit in," he said. "I didn't kill him."

"That doesn't explain how someone was able to swap sword when it was kept under lock and key," I said. "Unless you gave it to her directly as she didn't know you didn't work there."

"Someone else would've noticed if that were the case," Holmes shook her head. "Someone would have to know the place they were dealing with – am I right, Mrs McLaren?"

A hush fell over the room as everyone turned to the elderly woman. She grinned, holding her pipe in her mouth with her teeth.

"You're a fast pair, aren't you?" she said, taking the pipe out of her mouth and resting it on a shelf near her. Her expression was amused. She got to her feet and shuffled to the corner of the room.
"He was a monster and he deserved what he got," she said smiling. "I am glad I got to see it before I met my maker." Louise's head shot up. "What do you mean you got to see it?" For once in her life, Sherlock was impressed.

"Your grandmother's experience in the theatre meant she knew exactly where to go to find all the props," Holmes said glancing at me. "No doubt you had a key from your many years of service to the Adelphi, so it was just a matter of getting in."

Louise gasped as she snapped her head to Simeon. "You were in on this?" she gasped.
He shook his head frantically. "She wanted a word with him!" he exclaimed rubbing his head. "You know you can never say no to her."

The old woman gave us a toothy grin. "Damn right, you can't."

"Then it was just a matter of swapping the sword and waiting in a crate until the show began," Holmes said. "And you left during the madness of the performance when no one would notice you."

There was silence in the room.

"He was scum," Maggie spoke first, her back straightening proudly. "I believe I did a service." Despite my personal feelings that retribution had in fact been served, I knew the law wouldn't find it that way.

The family descended into madness, yet the old lady just resumed smoking her pipe. Happily content.

"How did you know it would work?" I asked. Then I thought of Healey and the Scottish play. "Unless you did it before."

Holmes and I shared a look – not surprise, as I was sure she had figured that out already.

"I had a friend die through his carelessness," Maggie said, suddenly solemn. "He was another of Abrams' kind – expected the world just because he was a man and said so." She breathed in deeply and then blew out rings. "So, I did it because I wanted to," she finished. "And for them."

After we solved the case, the elderly lady soon passed away. She had TB; it took her before she could be put to trial. Sherlock and I did pay tribute and saw the remaining properties and effects all went to Louise to ensure they could leave Devil's Acre and have more space for their children.

The sword in question appeared at our house one afternoon. It was incredibly light and Sherlock wouldn't tell me where it'd come from, only that she had tracked its history from a blacksmith's in Blackfriars. She kept it next to our fireplace and gave it a fitting name: Lady Macbeth.

The Theft of Evolution

It was a sunny Thursday in April when we were called to the Natural History Museum in South Kensington. I remember pulling up in our carriage and being struck by the beautiful masonry that seemed to gleam as if it were polished. Men in top hats, with beautiful ladies at their sides, waited patiently in a queue outside. The ladies' fans fluttered in bright colours. It looked so different under the brightness of the sky. The chatter of eager clients filled the air.

When the Museum had opened in the previous year of 1881, they had thrown a ball to celebrate. All members of high society were invited to the grand spectacle and left with minds filled to the brim with glories of the natural world and wonders of science. Sherlock had been invited, of course. I went along with her.

The gemstones were my favourite, there were thousands laid out in glass cabinets. Sherlock preferred the bones, however, and was on the prowl for the curator so she could ply him with questions on any history that she had ever been uncertain of. The rest of the time was spent avoiding Mycroft and his cronies from the government's higher offices, some of which I recognised from the Diogenes club. She did not elaborate, but I was sure some of them may have known Sherlock from the days before she adopted the moustache. She'd never been ashamed, but she did adopt an abashed look now and then if she was feeling particularly scandalous.

Today, families mused at all the exhibitions in the main hall. The skylight let the sun's rays stream down on all the glass cabinets that held every marvel away from the movement of time. Far from the gowns and tails of the night.

It was a unique and special day for all; the bustling crowds didn't seem to notice us as we slipped through eager patrons in order to get to the secure rooms at the back of the museum. I knew that, secretly, Sherlock was brimming with excitement. There was a skip in her walk and I had to take twice as many steps to keep up with her.

"Detectives! Thank goodness!" A bald man with a shiny forehead and dressed in a three-piece suit showed us to the scene of the crime. He introduced himself as Mr Beauchamp, museum creator and director, before sprinting off and we had to quicken again to follow him.

We were led to the archives under the museum where every manner of creature appeared to be jellied in jars. It sprawled outwards like a labyrinth of knowledge. The smell of cloistered air full of dust filled my lungs and I found myself spluttering. Ancient texts filled the space from floor to ceiling, scrolls, and manuscripts that outdated everyone in the room. The collection of bones, animals, and foreign relics seemed to go on forever. Sherlock's eyes were alight – it was like Christmas morning in Somberly manor had come sooner than expected.

"As you can see," the curator went on to say, "the museum is home to one of the largest collections of ancient academic texts in London, neigh, the better part of Europa." He walked us along to a cabinet in which a glass box lay smashed on the floor. Uniformed officers surrounded the area. I knelt to inspect it. The notation read as follows:

Editorial notes of Charles Darwin circa 1859.

My reading was more linked towards fiction, yet even I knew that name. I noticed Sherlock straighten immediately.

"Ah," Sherlock nodded. "No wonder the fuss."

"Darwin was a genius. There is no doubt about that," I added.

Mr Beauchamp mopped at his brow. "Yes, but some devil has stolen it!" His eyes were small in the rounded frame of his face, and currently wild with rage. His cheeks reddened. "I will see them shot!" Bits of spit flew everywhere; the man mumbled an apology before drawing out a lacy handkerchief.

I looked at the glass case and turned the corner to look further down the corridor at the rest of the collection. There were plenty of hand-written books, sculptures, figures, and drawings carefully protected in glass cases – a most impressive collection, indeed.

"You have a great collection of his work," Sherlock said, following me. The curator nodded but he was too upset to form words.

"Tell me, Sir." I turned back around. "Excluding the authorship, what makes this piece of work so important?"

Sherlock nodded. "Surely there are items are far more value in this archive."

The portly man started flailing his hands about his person.

"We are having a celebratory exhibition of Darwin's work commencing next month! This piece of work was cherished by him and I have it on good authority that Darwin's eager, academic flock would appear in numbers to see it." Beauchamp chewed on his fingernails and wiped his sweaty palms on his trouser legs.

"Have no fear, sir," Sherlock attempted to calm the frantic man, "I am sure we will find this work, and then you can resume with your exhibition as planned."
I smiled into a glove as I tried to keep a serious face. Sherlock couldn't deal with dramatic individuals – she said the drama was reserved for theatre only. Yet, this rule never appeared to apply to her. I think she quite enjoyed the spectacle.

"Certainly," Beauchamp said, clapping his hands together. "I am in the best hands! Holmes and Watson!"

Sherlock gave him a polite smile before she tipped her hat and sped off down the corridor like she had somewhere else to be. I turned to Beauchamp and went to shake his hand but instead, he dropped into a bow. I didn't know how to respond so I dipped my hat then sped in Sherlock's direction.

"Thoughts thus far?" I asked her once I had caught up.

"Only that it was very likely to be an inside job. No door has been reported broken, no lock tampered, no keys missing."

We stopped in a room with plenty of boxes in it. The space itself was big and filled to the brim. Each cargo crate seemed heavy and filled with some new object for the museum to show the world. The sliding door at the back must have been where they received deliveries. Sherlock and I shared a look and we instantly pried inside the nearest box – it looked big enough to fit a man inside, or perhaps a couple of children. Could this be the way the thieves had gotten in? Through one of the museum's guards, we discovered that they received deliveries once every fortnight. The stout man seemed to cower under Sherlock's cool gaze. Despite the makeup and the fake facial hair, it was intriguing to see how many gentlemen could lose themselves around her. We both couldn't hide a certain level of our femininity – some men found themselves quite confused indeed.

"Who controls what is being sent in?" Sherlock said, scouting around the boxes.

"That would be Beauchamp, Sir," the man confessed, his cheeks pinkening. He excused himself from our presence.

We found the portly curator languidly lying across some steps in the staff's quarter – as if the effort had been drawn out of him. He released a loud sigh as I approached him.

"When was the last delivery?" I asked him.

166

"Two nights hence," Beauchamp said, folding his arms.

Sherlock and I nodded. We started looking at the cargo boxes more intently and, sure enough, found a square wooden box with a loosened top. There was nothing inside besides some old newspapers and stuffing used to keep relics of the museum safe in transit.

"We are fairly confident that an individual came in here through delivery and then proceeded to snatch the book from its casing." Sherlock recapped, gripping her silver fox-head cane and tapping the box with it.

Beauchamp looked unwell and announced he needed to sit down. One of the museum's staff went to get him a glass of water and at some point he brandished a painted Japanese fan and started fanning himself with it.

"Goodness me," Sherlock whispered, raising her eyebrows. "Such a fuss over a book."

"Come now," I laughed. "I remember you made quite the fuss over getting your hands on a copy of *La Citoyenne*! Besides, you frequently make a fuss over some form of literature or another."

Sherlock put her nose in the air and rolled her eyes at me.

"Maybe you stole it," I teased. She looked at me, her blue eyes narrowed into slits. "You'd do anything to receive a good book."

"Within reason, of course. Expanding one's mind through knowledge is imperative towards growth, dear Watson." She winked at me and whispered into my ear, "You're rich to talk. I know the kind of filth you fill your head with. High horse, indeed, darling."
I flushed and walked off, leaving her among the jars of animal heads.

We inspected the staff areas and questioned each of them individually about their whereabouts and if they had seen anyone suspicious lurking in the archives. The place was so broad, and the archives so expanded, it seemed as if someone were to truly sneak in, they would've not been discovered for a while. Most had alibis easily backed up by other members of staff. So, even if the thief were one of them and others knew, the chances were that they wouldn't squeal on their colleagues.

We tracked down the original location of the last few boxes and arranged to meet the people who had transported the items in. They had unknowingly abetted a thief in stealing the book, which is ground enough for an arrest as being an accessory to the crime.

Beauchamp had already beat us to it. His voice bellowed down the halls like a boat's foghorn.

"You let a thief into my building! A thief! Who stole a book treasured by Charles Darwin himself!" He had turned a lobster-like shade, poising his fan at the oldest, flat-capped gentleman as if about to wallop him with it.

I readied myself for a fight. Sherlock simply rolled her eyes.

"Sir! There is no need to lose your temper in such a way," she sighed as she placed her open palm on her forehead.

"They may have not even been aware what cargo they were transporting," I added.

The tallest of the men was a tanned gentleman with black hair; his blue eyes were wide, and he had his hands in the air. He did not want to be hit by that fan.

"Mr Beauchamp! Sir! I can assure you, my colleagues and I had no idea! I swear! We just move them."

Much to our distaste, Mr Beauchamp could not seem to cease his tirade. The poor collection of movers gripped onto their caps tightly throughout the scolding. Perhaps a fight would've been easier to deal with. Sherlock's frown was deeply set – if her mother were still among us, she would've berated her for the expression and reminded her that it caused wrinkles.

I took the opportunity to inspect the mover's transport vehicle. The carriage was a box drawn by horses and kept undercover. One of the men who owned it told me everything was secured at the warehouse and they travelled by night. Thus, whoever boarded the vehicle had spent a night travelling before completing the theft. I winced. The box was too small to even raise one's head fully, their knees would have to be drawn to their chest. Unless the thief was a child, it would've been a very uncomfortable feat.

169

Sherlock left the rinsing of the movers to Beauchamp and joined me in inspecting the transport.

"Found anything, Detective?"

"I can't imagine an adult would've enjoyed being cramped in a tiny box for a whole day," I said. Sherlock shook her shoulders.

"They were determined. Unless it was a child."

A child might've been able to leave without being undetected, indeed. I could see Sherlock's nose wrinkled as she thought. I nudged her.

"Has the old brain come up with anything new?" I teased. "Or am I the only one with thoughts today."

Finally, she cracked a small smile and winked at me. "Ah, you tease," she giggled. "I have actually." She gestured to the wide archives. "There are so many treasures here! Ancient artefacts, relics, and precious stones that could sell for thousands with the right buyer." She pressed her palms onto the head of her cane. "As we have already said. Why take a book, even an important book like that, over the riches you could amass if you stole something else?"

She was right, of course. The museum had one of the biggest collections of natural stones in all of Great Britain. Diamonds, rubies, sapphires as big as your head were all boxed up and would've made very tidy pickings in the eyes of a thief.

"The natural conclusion that I have come to," she added, "is that it was stolen for semantic reasons rather than price."

We returned to Beauchamp when the yelling ceased and caught him dapping his head with his handkerchief. The fan was back too.

"Mr Beauchamp," I started. He turned to face me quickly as if I too were about to receive a verbal lashing. "We were curious about the origins of the piece – who possessed the book before it was sent here?"

The man took a few deep, cleansing breaths and drew the fan again slowly which he flapped.

"It was a gift from the Darwin estate itself. It was one of his prized possessions," he said mournfully before he resumed flapping the fan. "After the esteemed, Darwin's death," he continued, "the family's friend, Sir Joseph Dalton Hooker was given permission by his daughter to donate much of his work to scientific causes." Mr Beauchamp dabbed at his face with his handkerchief though he did not appear to be crying.

Sherlock hummed as she thought.

"Perhaps a disgruntled colleague wanted the book for themselves?" she posed. "I think it would be worth going to speak with this Dalton himself. Maybe the Darwins as well." At this Beauchamp's eyes went wide, his head frantically shaking. "Thoughts, Sir?" Sherlock pressed, eager to leave.

Beauchamp shrugged his shoulder and resumed flapping his fan as if he were an extension of his being.

"My previous interactions with the Darwins have been," he searched for the right word, "stifling, to say the least." He pursed his lips. "They possess no charisma, and they have no compassion." He shut the fan with a quick movement. "Gentlemen, as lovely as your company has been," the curator sighed, "I really must resume my curative duties! If you go and see my receptionist, who is in my office near the Prehistoric Exhibit, I am sure he can aid you in giving you details about the location of one Sir Joseph Dalton Hooker." He bowed to the pair of us once more before leaving the room in a swaying fashion as if he were wearing a gown.

I turned to Sherlock.

"That was an odd turn," I said. Sherlock nodded.

"Time to go and see what the Darwins are truly like, my dear."

It did not take us too long until we reached the upper surfaces once more. The Prehistoric exhibit was not too difficult to find either – it was marked at the entrance by a giant tusked beast with brown fur and a great long nose.

"Goodness, what a trunk!" I said, eyeing the mammoth.

"And other things you have never said," Holmes said with a grin.

We found a gentleman manning a desk near Beauchamp's and managed to get the details of Hooker and the Darwin family.

"I wonder why Beauchamp said those things about the Darwins," I looked to Sherlock, who was putting her top hat back on her head, straightening the collar on her cotton coat. "Bad blood perhaps?"

Sherlock breathed a sigh of relief as we stepped from the bustling halls of the museum into daylight. She glanced at the road ahead, then at me.

"Maybe," she wondered. "Let's go ask them, shall we?"

A carriage took us both to the edge of Knightsbridge to a small road called Ennismore Garden Mews. The houses were tall and made from a sandy coloured stone. The smell of jasmine and bay, wafting from the houses' gardens, filled the streets pleasantly. One could see through windows that the residents were enjoying a tipple of sherry or gin under the warming sunshine.

Number Eleven on this road had small baskets of flowers under the windows and pale white drapes hung from the windows which were wide open. We went and knocked the door to which an older gentleman opened. He had white hair and a beardy chin. His warm brown eyes were wide with the surprise of receiving us.

"Good afternoon, sir," I said, tipping my hat to him. "Are you Sir Hooker?"

The gentleman nodded.

"Yes! How may I help you, gentlemen?"

"I am Doctor Watson, and this is Detective Holmes – we are investigating a crime which we believed you might be able to aid us with."

"Goodness!" the man exclaimed, pushing the door open wide. "I recognise those names from the paper! Come in, gentlemen, come in!"

We stepped in through the door and the most wonderful smell filled my senses. Flowers were hanging from vases on every surface or held in bell jars or growing from pots. Gone was the soft scent of jasmine – this building smelled fresh like a greenhouse.

"Hyacinth, darling!" Hooker called to a white-haired lady in the rooms at the back. She wore a fitted day dress and a wide-brimmed straw hat on her head. The gentleman led us into the main room where there were chairs draped with red velvet. Flowers covered every surface imaginable.

The room was filled with natural light and what dominated the space was a mahogany, oval table, but even this was filled with books notes, scientific equipment, and Petri dishes. A cat stretched out by an open fire while a cage of coloured birds chirped away in the corner.

The woman then came into the room and dipped a curtsy for us.

"Detectives! I recognise your faces from the papers!" She clapped her hands together, excitedly. Her wrinkles made her beaming smile shine brighter. My heart sang as I smiled back. A pink tinge came to Sherlock's cheeks. "My husband and I do very much enjoy your stories in the paper! Especially all the grim murders," she said in a mock hush, coming to sit next to her husband on a seat near their open fire.

"Ah, yes," Hooker said, his tone soft and friendly. "The gorier the case – the more my lovely wife talks about it."

"Sit me down with a crime story and I'll be happy," she said. Her brown eyes twinkled. She cleared her throat.

"Speaking of which, how can we help you gentlemen?" Hooker said, knitting his fingers together in his palms.

I turned to look at Sherlock. She nodded and rested her hands on the top of her cane.

"You were the close friend of Charles Darwin, is that correct?" she asked. The old gentleman nodded. "One of his notebooks was recently stolen from the Natural History Museum – we were curious to know if there were any parties that were in this particular notebook?"

Sherlock described the notebook in question to which the gentleman looks surprised.

175

"Goodness! If you were referring to the notebook I think you are referring to – then I am surprised it was in the possession of the museum at all," Sir Hooker exclaimed. "That notebook belonged to his daughter, Henrietta."

"Was it precious to her?" I asked.

"Yes, very much so indeed," he replied. "Now someone has stolen it? I wonder for what purpose? It is just notes and scribblings about his now published work."

"So, you would say it's not valuable?" Sherlock pressed her lips together.

Hooker gestured with his hands as he spoke. "Charles was a splendid man, and his work is famed around the globe. Thus, I believe someone would buy it, but to the untrained eye it wouldn't be worth two shillings. Nothing more than a diary."

His expression became clouded like it was wound up in memories.

Hyacinth served us some tea before we had even had the chance to politely refuse it. We learned that Hooker was a botanist and even now, when he had retired, still studied plants in the comfort of his home. Which explained the greenhouse that was in fact their living room.

"Have you spoken much to Henrietta recently, dear?" Hyacinth asked her husband.

Hooker took a sip of his tea and shook his head. "Not recently, dear. I heard from her mother that she and her husband, that amiable fellow Litchfield, are off on another one of their tours across the west country."

After that, Hyacinth made a note of the residence of Miss Darwin and handed it to me. The pair requested that we come around for tea whenever it was convenient. Which we had no choice but to agree. They waved from the doorstep as we summoned a carriage to take us back to Baker Street.

The hour was late, so we believed it to be prominent to rest until the morn. It was then we would venture to Gomshall, a little town in Surrey, where Henrietta and her husband lived. Sherlock was lecturing me on the importance of making a good impression, like I was the one who did not behave in social situations.

"Because, *John*," she adjusted the fuchsia satin gloves she wore, "the Darwins are one of those families I believe are destined to be a household name and you know how much I crave to learn about science." Her expression was smug. This was her way in. She probably had a list of questions tucked into one of her pockets somewhere. "Imagine all the scientific minds we could meet! And the acquaintances we could make!"

"You loathe parties," I said as I crossed my arms. "You called everyone at the Princess' last birthday party a *collection of royal farts in wigs and waistcoats.*"
I drew in a breath and felt my lungs sit uncomfortably in my chest. I must've bound too tightly. I did not miss the tightness of the corset; it seemed that in order to be an appropriately

177

dressed woman I would need to sacrifice any ability to breathe. It did not seem fair as men did not have to wrestle themselves into anything. Being a woman was more complicated than the Gordian knot.

Comfort was a compromise I would only make for Sherlock. Not like she needed a corset with a waist that naturally small. She hid her smile behind an embroidered fan.

"Yes, that does seem like something I would say," she concurred. "Do not misunderstand me, John. I do loathe parties when they are held by dull people."

"Even rich ones?" I asked. They threw extravagant affairs like money was no consequence. Sherlock never held back when it came to celebrating her birthday – or mine for that matter.

"You could be as rich as the queen," she sighed, pulling up her glove, "but if you as dull as a dustbin, I shall not come."

The carriage drew up at the village of Gomshall.

"Take Wilde for example. He is not made of money at all, despite what he likes to think. Yet he throws the most wonderful parties and I always leave feeling intellectually stronger."

Wilde was one of the most eccentric people I had ever met. Hedonism at its finest – but he held a room so well. I nodded in agreement.

"He is a Wilde one," I said. Sherlock swatted me with her fan.

We finally drew up at the house that Hyacinth had written on the note and ascended the stairs to a small, red-bricked property. I went first and knocked. I heard footsteps from behind the door before a middle-aged woman opened it.

"Hello," she said, her eyes wide. "How may I help you?"

She had dark eyes that we deeply set in her face and long, brown hair that was plaited into a bun at the back of her head. Her face was rounded with pinked cheeks. She wore a blue dress with a laced collar.

I cleared my throat. It was a shame but some of this would need to be a façade to protect our working identities.

"Hello, are you miss Henrietta Litchfield - whose father was Charles Darwin?" I asked. The woman was visibly taken aback.

"Yes, he was my father," she said, her voice was light. "I am sorry – who are you?"
Sherlock smiled as gracefully as ever and lowered her hood. "My name is Sherlock Holmes, and this is my companion Doctor Watson." Henrietta's dark eyes lit up and her hand flew to her mouth. She dipped a curtsy. Her face framed in shock. Sherlock continued, "We are here on official police business about a notebook belonging to your father – can we come in?"

Henrietta immediately drew the door wide and ushered us into a square room with each wall made of shelves filled with books. I saw the same situation in the next one.

"An avid reader, are we?" I asked Henrietta.

She smiled bashfully, gripping her hands together at the front. "My husband and I are editors. A lot of his work comes home with him and we work on it together."

Sherlock looked about the shelves intently. Her library was about seventeen times the size of this one, so she was probably looking for her favourites.

"What are the pair of you are doing here? What did the detectives want to know?" Henrietta asked, folding her hands on her lap as she sat down.

We explained the situation, exchanging our names for our detective ones, of course. Henrietta's face changed throughout our story. She placed a hand on her mouth as we finished.

"Goodness me!" she gasped. "So, it was stolen." She drew a breath, looking at the floor. It seemed her shoulders were shaking. Henrietta pressed her hands to her knees over her skirts.

"Are you alright, miss?" I asked. Sherlock's eyes narrowed.

The lady blew out a breath then shook her head. She excused herself a moment and disappeared. We heard some shuffling as gentle footsteps ascended the stairs. A few moments later she returned with an armful of notebooks. Pulling one from the bunch, she laid it out separately from the others. I looked at it closely and noted the descriptions scribbled on the front. The dogeared nature of the book confirmed it.

"Before you say anything, I did not know it was stolen," she said, picking it up gingerly. "It was returned to me a couple of days ago with a note from my husband saying that it was given back to him at the museum after he completed his research for the Telegraph there on the new Prehistoric Exhibition." She continued, telling us the book had belonged to her during her father's writing of *Descent of Man*. She edited lots of his work and Mr Darwin had valued her support before his work was published.

"This notebook was precious to me," Henrietta confessed. "After my father died lots of his things and his research were donated to good causes." She shook her head passionately. Her face drew in a stern expression. "But I would never give this up! On the night of the charity auction, this was stolen from my house." She pulled another one of the books from the pile. It seemed to be her own diary. "Look, see here! My handwriting is the same!" Even an untrained eye could see the similarity. She flipped through a different book and pulled a page from a newspaper clipping. It was a reward for the lost book to be returned to one Henrietta Litchfield.

I felt the old clipping in my hands. The paper had been pressed smooth by the pages of her diary. I could hear the wobble in her voice.

"Forgive me, sirs," she said, sincerely. "I am sorry for any grief that has been caused. I truly am. But I am happy this has been returned to me, through whatever means! Tell the detectives that I will fight tooth and nail to keep this book."

Sherlock and I exchanged a look. "When you explained this to the curator, what did he say?"

Henrietta scowled, her fists clenched by her sides. She stormed off into the hallway and returned with a letter marked by the stamp of the museum.

"He refused," she said, gritting her teeth. "He said he had documents signed that approve our donating them. I did not know that he had put in that notebook too."
Sherlock nodded her head. Her face was unreadable.

"You realise your husband must've stolen or hired someone to steal this back for you?" I spoke ."Where is he now?"

"Yes. I understand and I'm so thankful to him." Her grin was wide as her eyes sparkled with tears. "He is in Edinburgh doing contract work for a publisher. I daresay he won't be back for weeks."

Sherlock nodded and we both shared the same thought. "Would you mind accompanying us to London, dear?" she asked, her face bright and full of determination. "We have a mess to sort out and a criminal to convict."

We took Henrietta to London and had the lads in Scotland Yard take her statement. We changed our attires during this period. Upon returning to the station, we found a white-faced Beauchamp fleeing from the scene.

Miraculously, the charges were dropped, and Henrietta was allowed to keep her book. And as a sign of goodwill, she and the rest of her descents were granted free entry to the National History Museum.

Henrietta had also figured us out, but swore she would keep our secret.

"How did you guess?" I asked with a grin.

She held onto her bonnet as the wind swept through Hyde Park. Her smile was graceful and she pinkened at the cheeks.

"You are too refined for men," she replied.

Sherlock pulled a face, "We shall work on it."

I could only smile.

The Missing Ward of Sir Olivier

Sir Olivier Meads was a renowned musician with a reputation as spotless as the ivory keys of his famous grand piano. Sherlock and I had the pleasure of seeing him perform at Yuletide the year prior. He had played all the classics and had everyone sing hymns.

As a young lady of society, Sherlock Holmes had been meticulously trained in all endeavours ladylike and proper. That included the gentle art of musical instruments – the piano being one of her greatest "loathes" as she claimed. Though she could play well, she hated performing for anyone – apart from me, of course. But Sir Olivier couldn't be more different – he relished the spotlight. Composing book after book of music for people to play. And, on rare occasion, taking young men and women as his protegees in hopes that they, too, would master the art on which he prided himself so.

That was how he'd come to be known amongst society. Sherlock and I, however, knew him to be an odious fellow with leering eyes and wide ambitions to marry well. Unfortunately for him, he had not been blessed much in terms of appearances. Meads rather looked like a toad. His greyish skin was always clammy with sweat, his eyes were set round and agog in his head. Naturally, women were in quite the short supply around him.

Detective Holmes and I were called to his London home late one evening in August. The applying of our male guises was done mostly in the candle-lit darkness and had meant our moustaches were glued a little more askew than usual. Upon arrival, we were shown into Sir Meads' study – a grand room with an arched ceiling, like a chapel, and a great desk made of mahogany wood.

"Sir Meads, we are not uniformed officers and do not take well to being summoned without ample reason," Sherlock started. When we had received the call, we had already readied ourselves for bed. We had been specifically requested, however, and, due to the upper-class calibre of the caller, Commissioner Clarke couldn't refuse the call.

Sir Meads wore a dinner suit, his greying hair was oiled into a stiff brushed position on his head. His chin was darkened by his beard shadow and he smelled fresh, in need of a bath. He grimaced at Holmes' words.

"Good detectives, I apologise for the lateness, but my case is of the most urgency." He shook Sherlock's hand and then mine. I winced at the dampness and tried to discreetly wipe it away. "I need to report a missing person."

I looked to Sherlock, then back at Sir Meads. Her eyes were fixed as she gripped her cane in annoyance.

"Forgive me, *Sir*," I said, through gritted teeth, "is that the reason why we have been summoned here? That is a matter that could've been reported directly to the station."

Sir Meads was quick to dismiss me. "Detective, I do not care for your tone," he said, raising his nose at me. "I asked for the services of the pair of you specifically as this problem requires the highest order of secrecy and must be kept out of the public eye at all costs!" He gestured to the chaise opposite him. We sat down.

185

I noticed the smell of liquor in the air and the redness in his eyes. The blood vessels in his cheeks were aglow as if he were cold. His lips were chapped too.

"I have a ward – my sister's child, who resides here with me while her husband is in the Americas," he told us, gripping his hands together. "She is not the easiest to live with – she throws rowdy parties with her friends and even has," he cleared his throat, looking about the room as if he were searching for the right word among the plush chairs of the room before whispering, "male companions."

I could see Sherlock's eyes roll through the side of my vision.

"Sir, I'm afraid you have misjudged us. If you think we are available to hire to solve family problems – then you are gravely mistaken." That was true enough. I could barely get Sherlock to talk to her own family; Mycroft was as prickly to her as a holly bush.

Sir Meads' expression hardened.

"Detective Holmes, I was told that you and Watson were the best in your field. Am I going to have to tell everyone that the pair of you are the worst? Perhaps I should've called your brother?"

There were enough rumours about us as it was. I was certain the son of a Duke's word wouldn't do well to our reputation. Meads took our chagrin as his own triumph.

186

"Excellent," he clapped his hands. "Now, Lily must be found and returned here with the utmost discretion."

He told us that the last night he had seen her, she had just come in from a riotous night, he was sure, at one of her friends' house. The friend in question was one Lady Agatha Buckingham – a scandalous woman with thoughts, feeling, and, woe betide, ideas! Could you ever imagine? Sir Mead said they had fought upon Lily's arrival home. She had been most vicious when he'd scolded her about spending money.

"She thinks that we have gallons of it! Drinks it away!" he exclaimed, shaking his head. Sherlock's expression was steely. Lily had fled into the night like a "harlot bat" and had not been seen in a week. Mr Meads didn't care for the child overly, however, he would have very much liked his money back. Which she stole upon her departure.

"If she is a thief, this is more reason to call the police," I said. "A force could be monopolised in order to find her."

Meads shook his head and groaned, then proceeded to slam his fist down onto the table. I jumped up and whatever part of me that was hoping for a quick return to bed was quickly put down.

"Watson, are you a dim-witted, condescending berk? We have been over this. I cannot be seen having her had my ward!"

Holmes did not flinch, but raised her chin indignantly. "If you did not want anyone to know she was here, why did you permit her to leave?" she asked, leaning forwards.

"Gossip in upper circles spreads like wildfire among dry grass. The chances are that they already know."

The man's face deepened into a scowl. He spoke very slowly and poised one finger at Sherlock and I.

"You will continue with the utmost discretion." His eyes narrowed. "Or else."

I saw Sherlock's jaw tense. The grip on her cane tightened.

"We will find her," Holmes said. The gent frowned. "Sir."

Meads sent me a look of warning.

"We will," I added quickly.

"Do it well, gentleman and you will be compensated," he sniffed. "It can't be much – a detective's salary."

I was nearly certain that Sherlock's allowance was probably double, if not triple what this puffed and powdered fool kept in the tightness of his purse strings.

After reluctantly heeding Sir Mead's words, we took to London to see if we could find Miss Lily Meads. Firstly, we enquired about the location of Lady Agatha Buckingham, but when we called the estate, they told us she had gone away for the week to attend the races in Gloucester. The servants reported that she had gone with her husband alone and a collection of her friends. None of which included the name, Lily Meads.

With our first lead evaporated, we started in the West End and headed to the dodgiest of taverns and clubs that lay between the high streets. It seemed to surprise Sherlock that I knew some of the bar owners there. In my years of medical training at St Bartholomew's, I had done pretty much anything I could to fit in; sometimes that meant antics that left me red-faced upon reflecting on them.

We weaved our way through town and asked for any young ladies of noble birth, but we were met with jokes about bedding a woman of worth. Holmes was quick to remind them that they were not worth any woman if they judged one on such menial qualities. Little known to them I already had a woman of worth.

Sherlock was bristled by Sir Meads' behaviour and kept an iron countenance as we explored the shadows and opium dens of London's gin-intoxicated streets. The streets were covered in mud and public waste. These parts of our city were not as well kept as the clean streets near the place. Children sat by open fires and huddles under rags.
She and I regularly donated to the poor and to charity schools. But I knew it wounded her when she saw whole families living on the street, struggling in poverty in the rat-infested hovels they had built themselves. She couldn't bear to look, keeping her eyes on her boots.

I gave the change I had in my pockets to a small boy with hair cut close to the skin. He had coal smeared on his cheeks and his fingers were black with soot. I felt my heart

189

turn heavy in my chest. He mumbled his thanks before running off into the night.

"I could get you a noble lady, gentlemen," a man announced coming up behind us. He had teeth that looked like he gnawed on tobacco for a living. His burgundy coat was stained and torn at the hem and he wore a top had that was filled with feathers.

"No, thank you," Sherlock said, walking by. The gentleman made a whistling noise and from the shadows emerged a group of men. Silence fell around us with the incoming steps of boot crunching on mud. Sherlock made sure I was behind her. "Can we help you, gentlemen?"

"Give us all your valuables," the rodent-looking man said. He tugged on his coat and placed his hands in his pockets. "Or we'll happily remove your kidneys from your person."

Sherlock only smiled politely.

I saw the glint of a dagger in one man's hand. Another had a hand in his coat pocket, ready to draw a weapon of his own.

I heard the click of Sherlock's cane. It had been crafted by a close friend of hers. When done properly, the cane could separate and, much to my delight, become two rapiers.

"Apologies, Sir," she spoke. "That will not happen. Give up now or we'll happily remove more than your kidneys from your person."

A few of the men chuckled nervously. The rest stiffened.

"Come now, gentlemen," he said, patting his pocket. "The bobbies must be paying the best detectives on the force a pretty penny."

"You are very much mistaken," I said, making a note of where everyone was. Sherlock's breaths were short, her movements careful, as she readied to divide the weapon. "We may be the best, but truthfully, the bawds of London make better money than we ever could."

Sherlock chuckled, but the men did not find my joke amusing. Slowly one stepped forward – this seemed to be the signal as the rest came upon us with vigour. My companion then divided her cane and handed me a rapier; the top was tied with a red ribbon as Sherlock's own was the fox head cane topper. The man with the dagger yelled as he approached. She swung her weapon with force and slit a long cut in the back of his hand, deep enough to bring out a yell from him, causing him to drop the knife.

The other gentleman, who had something in his pocket, drew out a rusty knife. His companion ran towards me and swung to punch me in the face. I ducked out of the way and used his vulnerable arm that he had just so carelessly swiped in the air to throw him at the knife wielder. Neither of them had predicted that I would use their own force against them. The rogue knife stabbed into the first man's shoulder. He howled – a delightful sound, I must admit – and, in shock, the wielder drew the knife out in haste, Causing the first man to scream and then run off.

The knife-wielder now covered in his companion's blood attempted another swing at me. Adrenaline filled my veins as I thrust one hand up, under his jaw, feeling the bone crack with the force. The man was stunned and instantly dropped the knife before passing out at my feet.

Sherlock handled the other villains with a delicate precision that one can only equate to needlework if the needle were a deadly rapier. She kicked one man in the face while elbowing another in the groin. The sounds of their discomfort was music to my ears!

"Goodness, is that all?" Sherlock wheeled in the balls of her feet. Her coat spun around her. I handed back the blade and she reassembled her cane.

"It seems to be." The men were unmoving in their states of unconsciousness. "A quick finish."

Sherlock smirked, the hair of her fake moustache crinkling.

We composed ourselves once more and headed into the dirty streets, turning into a nearby tavern in the early hours of the morning. Everyone who had enough wits was back in their bed at this time – that didn't mean the streets were not full of night people.

At the bar, we enquired about Lily Meads.

"What do you want with her, gentlemen?" the barmaid asked, an Irish lilt on her tongue. Her cheeks were rouged – perhaps with powder or maybe of the sheer heat generated by the throng of so many bodies cramped into a tiny space. She had red hair plaited across her head and, apart from her cheeks, her skin was the colour of milk. "She is the daughter of a lady, after all. Why would she be in these parts?"

"We are enquiring the whereabouts of Miss Meads at the behest of her uncle, Sir Meads," Sherlock explained. "She has been missing for a few days and he is concerned that she is in trouble."

The barmaid paused serving people and cast a look to her busy colleagues. She swiped her hands on her apron, opened the bar door, and ushered us through to the back.

"Lily frequents these bars with her man friend – I know the pair of them. His name is Tobias Ignacio, works in the cobblers over on Portobello road." She put her hands on her hips, forehead wrinkling.

"She had plans to marry him in the future, but I know they were waiting until her allowance came through."

I shook my shoulders.

"Maybe she and this Ignacio fellow eloped?" I wondered aloud. Sherlock raised an eyebrow.

The barmaid's brown eyes landed on me and narrowed. Her fingers curled into a fist at her side.
"She wouldn't dare," she said with finality. "No. Something foul must have happened."

Sherlock caught my eye and I saw the corner of her mouth twitch. "I am sorry. We didn't ask your name," she said, her gaze focused. Finally, we had a lead we could follow.

"Aoife Sparrow, sirs." Aoife flounced one hand in the air like she was going to perform a fancy curtsy, but she bowed instead. "No need to ask your names – how do you ever solve crimes, being on every page of The Strand yourselves?" "A fair question," Sherlock replied. "Not everyone reads The Strand. Plus, dear Watson and I are masters of disguise."

At this Aoife snorted. "Sure, you are," she giggled, her laughter was as melodious as a windchime. "I would like to see the pair of you in a woman's clothes."

"Many people would," I said, winking at Sherlock who rolled her eyes in response.

Aoife agreed to meet us at noon the following day to find this Ignacio man. He worked during the night and she didn't know where it was. We would confront him on Lily's whereabouts then. The barmaid was certain that he knew something. According to her, there was little he did without Lily's approval. According to her, it was sickening to see the pair in action.

In the middle of the day, Portobello Road was full of sellers from all over, flogging their wares to anyone who would listen. Punnets of plumbs. Lengths of lace. Cuts of cheese. The hollering went on and on and on.

I yawned into the back of my hand and Holmes had dark rings under her eyes.

194

"Come on, come on! We don't have all day now!" a tired Aoife appeared behind us and swept us down the road. She wore an embroidered shawl over her plain green frock. "My friend needs to be found and find her we shall!"

Marshall's Cobblers lay behind the colourful striped tents of the market. A single window was painted with the image of a shoe, and fanciful lettering pointed out the shop's opening times, as well as the managers of the place. Before we could stop her, Aoife kicked the door wide open with one brown boot.

"Tobias Ignacio! Where are you? I need a word!" she yelled at the top of her lungs, scaring the soul out of the older gentleman fitting some leather over a shoe. His mouth dropped, frozen in shock. His pipe clattered to the floor. Even Sherlock was taken aback. Aoife yelled his name again. She truly was a foghorn of a woman.

A man wearing leather gloves emerged from behind a door in the back. His face was tanned, his dark hair shining under the lamplight as did his squared jaw. He was attractive, indeed, but his expression was murderous.

"What in the nine realms of hell is wrong with you?" He said something, I believe in Spanish, to the gentleman, still stunned in his seat, who then abandoned his work and left the room post-haste. "Can you be any louder? I felt like my mother could hear you in Heaven!" He spied us like he had just noticed this fiery Irish woman was not alone. "And who are these men you have brought here?"

"Detectives Holmes and Watson, obviously." Aoife was undeterred. She stepped closer and narrowed her eyes, raising one finger, and prodded Ignacio squarely in the chest. "Lily. Where is she?" she barked accusingly, resuming the prodding in his chest. The man slapped her hand away, causing her scowl to deepen.

"I don't know where she is," Ignacio responded. He crossed his arms and the muscles in them moved with the motion. Aoife shook her head and put her hands on her hips. "The hell you don't!" her voice went up an octave. We all winced.

Tobias sighed.

"I'm guessing she didn't tell you then," he said in a low tone. "Things are dead between us."

Aoife huffed and rolled her eyes. Surely, a familiar reflex to a regular occurrence.
"What lovers' tiff have I walked into now?" she sighed. Tobias shook his head and rubbed his brow with his right hand.

"No, Aoife! It's gone – over – kaput!" he kept shaking his head. He turned from us and walked into the back of the store. There was a clatter of noise before he returned with gusto. "She made it very clear to me that things are over between us." Tobias handed Aoife a letter before folding his arms and leaning back on the table.

Aoife inspected the piece, pausing her tirade for a moment. Sherlock and I hovered behind her. Despite only making out a few words, the letter's pretty, clear font meant I could gather the gist of its contents. Lily had left Tobias for another man. They were eloping and she was sorry for all the grievance she had caused. Sherlock and I shared a look. It said she was heading for India to start a new life. There was a signature at the bottom. I meant to ask Aoife if we could have it once she had read it in order to pair check it with another of her letters. Suddenly, there was a scrunch of paper. I accidentally gasped as the barmaid belled the evidence and thrown at Tobias' head.

"Tobias," Aoife hissed, severely disappointed. "There is no way Lily wrote that letter."

Tobias' expression was frozen, his eyes wide at the now balled up letter on the ground. He looked to us and then back to Aoife.

"Come on! Lily's handwriting looks as if a spider jumped into an inkpot then onto a page!" Aoife continued. "It's nearly unreadable!"

"The letter was written in a very neat hand," Holmes remarked.

Tobias' expression lit up. "Wait does this mean –" he started. Aoife nodded.

"She's not left you, lad. Even though she should, because you're a clod."

With that, it seemed the drama had passed. Sherlock and I found our voices again.

"When was the last place you saw her, Mr Ignacio?" she asked. Tobias straightened up.

"She was dropped off at her apartment in Mayfair. She planned to stay there until the drama had passed with her uncle."

"Drama?" I pressed. "What happened?"

Tobias clenched his jaw and his fists. "Her creepy uncle has always been odd around young women. He behaved inappropriately toward Lily, asking her to come to his bed. Asking for *other things* too." Aoife's jaw steeled tight. Tobias didn't look any of us in the eye, he looked as if he were shaking. "Then he decided that he was entitled to her inheritance, too. Lily was furious. She left for her mother's old apartment and was quite happy there when I last saw her a couple of evenings ago. Her uncle didn't know about it – he couldn't find her there.
"

"But why write the letter?" Aoife said folding her arms. "Why bother ruining a relationship out of spite?"

Tobias immediately threw his overcoat over his leather apron. "Because someone wanted me out of the way."

Sherlock hoisted her cane in the air. "To the estate."

We immediately caught a taxi to Mayfair, conquering the last few streets on foot. Tobias took us in through a back way that involved hopping over a fence. He did it easily, but Aoife struggled, swearing nosily as she did so. He told us, with a cheeky smirk, that this way avoided the footmen. We snuck in through a window that landed us in one of the informal drawing rooms. The door was ajar as Tobias lead us through up to another tall white door with golden decoration.

"Lily?" he spoke gently, pushing the door open. A sight of disarray met us. Her room was a state – it had been nearly destroyed. The bed's sheets were ripped, the curtains yanked from their poles, clothes littered the floor. Plates and what I assumed was a vase had been thrown in a smashed pile at the bottom of the bed. Tobias straightened up and went over to the jewellery table, picking up a delicate silver bangle. "This was her favourite – she never went anywhere without it."

It was also one of the few things that had been left in its original state.

"Then Sir Meads has something to do with it," Holmes said. She threw me a look – we both had the same thought.

"She must be here," I said.

We quickly and quietly looked through the other rooms on this floor. Neither Meads, nor Lily were to be found. If we were caught here without good reasoning, we were going to be in an even worse situation.

Perhaps she was not here. Why would Sir Mead call us if he had her himself? None of it made any sense.

All of a sudden, a tiny female maid with her hair tied up in a bonnet turned a corner and gasped, dropping a tray of old teacups. The lot smashed, causing a ruckus. We all held our breaths collectively. As her bright blue eyes met mine, I raised my hands.

"Please don't scream," I whisper-yelled. "We're police!"

The lady froze and lowered her gaze to the floor.

"Agatha?" Tobias questioned. Turning to us, he said, "This is Lily's handmaid."
The lady gave Tobias a long mournful look.

"Do you know anything about her whereabouts, ma'am?" Holmes inquired. "We're worried for her safety."

The maid clasped her hands together and for a brief moment, there was a torn look on her face. Then she caved and spoke.

"The wine cellar," she stuttered, eyes watering. "He's gone mad. I think he's going to kill her."

As Tobias charged forward, I entrusted the maid to call the Yard, requesting backup for Holmes and Watson in order to apprehend a villain. Then we bolted towards the cellar. At some point, Aoife had grabbed a thin blade – no more than a letter opener and was wielding it as if it were a sword.

The lower floor was empty. I assumed Sir Meads had given the staff the night off to accomplish the deed. I only prayed we were not too late. The wine cellar was the size of our whole flat. Shelves upon shelves of bottles, barrels, and canisters of alcohol from all over the world. The air inside was cold and smelled damp and ancient.

"Lily!" Tobias yelled. "Lily, where are you?"

A beat passed in silence. Then – a gunshot. Tobias flew back into a set of shelves, causing the bottles to crash to the floor. He lost his footing and fell beside the glass. A high-pitched scream echoed through the space. It happened so quickly I could barely process it. Aoife picked up a bottle of wine and threw it with unimaginable force in the direction of where the shot had come from before she dived toward Tobias. There was a great smash and a clunk as a body fell to the floor with a groan. We edged out and saw a scene as if from a piece of horror literature. Tied up high and resting on her toes was a lithe terribly pale figure, blonde locks falling limp around her. Her lips were white. I wondered how long she had been dehydrated.

It was a malicious act – Meads was planning on letting her starve and die here while torturing her while she was still alive, no doubt about it.

The red wine bottle that Aoife had thrown smashed upon Meads. She must've gotten the back of his neck. The wine had made the red of his blood look even more horrifying. I quickly checked him while Holmes released the girl from her bonds. I reused the rope to bind Mead's hands.

The girl came round from her stupor and her eyes found her friends.

"Tobias? Aoife?" she croaked, stumbling forward into Aoife's arms, who received her with a sob. The barmaid lightly, yet tearfully berated her for causing trouble.

I checked Tobias and found he'd been shot in the shoulder. I quickly wound my scarf around the wound in order to get some pressure on it until we could take him to the hospital.

"They won't believe you," Meads grumbled as he came round and realised his predicament. "I am a Lord! You are a nobody."

"Maybe," Holmes said as Lestrade barged in, flanked by officers. "But I don't believe you have many friends that will vouch for you, *sir*."

"Evening, boys." Lestrade clapped Holmes on the back. He looked down at the wine-covered noble and pressed his lips together. "You'll never guess," he added. "We've just had this man's entire household at the station, reporting him for abuse and abduction."

I turned to Holmes and I could not ignore the urge to smile.

"Oh my," Holmes said. "That is interesting."

The maid in the corner smiled then.

Also from Orange Pip Books

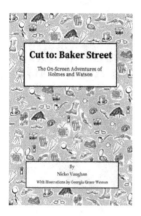

It is well documented that Sherlock Holmes is the most depicted literary character on screen; he even has an entry in the Guinness Book of Records to prove it. This reference guide covers depictions of the world's most famous detective, and his faithful companion, from the first silent film Sherlock Holmes is Baffled (1900) to the Will Ferrell, John C. Reilly comedy Holmes and Watson (2018). As well as cinema and television portrayals, this book by Nicko Vaughan (Author of The Wordy Companion: An A-Z Guide to Sherlockian Phraseology) also covers documentaries, animations and web series adaptations alongside début feature artwork by graphic artist Georgia Grace Weston.

Combining encyclopaedia, biography and reference structure, this book comprehensively explores the many celluloid faces, cathode-ray shapes and digital sizes of Sherlock Holmes and Doctor John Watson, so far.

Also from Orange Pip Books

Violet Holmes is not an ordinary teenager because, well, nothing is ordinary when you're the adopted daughter of the great Sherlock Holmes. Having been home schooled for her entire life she has decided to take the plunge, at 14, and attend Bardle Secondary School to study for her exams. But after a week, she notices that the school hides a deep secret, and she's determined to crack it wide open. Are the current spate of school thefts the work of criminal masterminds? Is there really a secret society behind closed doors? Can a girl like Violet make friends and fit in?

Also from Orange Pip Books

Just the place for a Nark!" the Detective cried,

As he eagerly surveyed the scene;

With the stout-hearted Doctor alert at his side,

And the Dog standing guard in between.

Imagine a world where the logic of Sherlock Holmes meets the nonsense of Wonderland! *The Hunting of the Nark* combines the best of Lewis Carroll and Arthur Conan Doyle's adventures into a madcap collection of verse, including the novella-length case, *The Adventure of the Twinkling Hat*. Holmes and Watson will discover that anything can happen at 221B when you're the White Knight...

Also from Orange Pip Books

Dr. John H. Watson is a man of medical science, a man of action and a man of letters. His life has been one of adventure and romance. In 1894 he finds himself alone following the death of his great friend Sherlock Holmes three years earlier and now the passing of his beloved wife, Mary. His loneliness is all encompassing and only a true friend can help him to see there is still reason to continue living. But when that friend, Inspector G. Lestrade of Scotland Yard suddenly and mysteriously disappears, Dr. Watson takes it upon himself to discover the reason for the abduction.

Also from Orange Pip Books

It wasn't that John couldn't tell the story. It wasn't that we didn't know the truth. It was that nobody would believe us. But we cannot keep Sherlock alive with silence. The reader smiles when Moriarty appears on the page. So does Moriarty. And Sherlock Holmes follows him. We smile because we recognise them. Scarlett Vendalle is recognised by nobody, except for John Watson. With no recollection of her own identity and a suspected criminal past, Scarlett is the perfect case for Sherlock. As they follow her tracks, red threads appear in their lives that make it more than clear - Scarlett meeting John and Sherlock was no coincidence. Someone has drawn her shadow on the wall before she appeared. Was it Anne Boleyn who haunts Scarlett with visions of her past? Was it Moriarty who attracts Sherlock like a magnet? Or was it another shadow from the past? With Moriarty's men on the one hand and the secret service on the other, the stage is set for a game with deadly rules, as Sherlock, John and Scarlett slowly become aware that something larger is guiding their steps...
Is there another story being written...?

Also from Orange Pip Books

On New Year's Day 1891, Sherlock Holmes summons the limping street urchin, Wiggins, to Baker Street and decrees he must die at dawn. Wiggins, however, has other plans. To fulfil the dying wish of his mother, Irene Adler, he schemes with his two formidable American aunties to keep two important facts from the great detective: Mrs. Hudson is actually his Aunt Grizelda, and he is both Holmes' child and a girl pretending to be a boy. Through a series of mysterious letters Adler bequeathed to Wiggins, the dark backstory of her parents and all their long-kept family secrets unravel. To flee the mad King of Bohemia trying to claim Wiggins as his heir, Holmes and Wiggins begin their Great Hiatus. From Mycroft to Moriarty, from Dr. John H. Watson to the Baker Street Irregulars, from P.T. Barnum to Jumbo the Elephant, Wiggins learns little is what it seems. Slowly learning to trust each other, Holmes and Wiggins travel from London to Reichenbach Falls to New York City to a small farm in Canada which holds the secrets of their family history. Together, they correct the errors in Watson's tales, bond over Wiggins' disability, drop their masquerades, and deduce a father and daughter future.

Also from Orange Pip Books

Janey Wiggins lives a desperate life in London's East End at the end of the nineteenth century. With little education and fewer prospects, she has no hope of escaping the grinding poverty, constant hunger, and ever-present danger of life on the street -- that is, until a chance meeting with the great detective Sherlock Holmes and his friend Dr. Watson. Hired on as Holmes's apprentice "irregular," Janey turns her adversity to her advantage. As she and her friends investigate the mysterious appearance of a ghost in the upper window of a local home, Janey discovers how important she can be. But when her theory of the case clashes with Holmes's and a child's life may be on the line, will she find the courage to act?

CPSIA information can be obtained
at www.ICGtesting.com
Printed in the USA
LVHW052113200921
698283LV00012B/365